Marion's Angels

K. M. PEYTON
Marion's Angels

Illustrated by
Robert Micklewright

OXFORD UNIVERSITY PRESS
Oxford   New York   Toronto   Melbourne
1979

Oxford University Press, Walton Street, Oxford

OXFORD   LONDON   GLASGOW
NEW YORK   TORONTO   MELBOURNE   WELLINGTON
KUALA LUMPUR   SINGAPORE   JAKARTA   HONG KONG   TOKYO
DELHI   BOMBAY   CALCUTTA   MADRAS   KARACHI
NAIROBI   DAR ES SALAAM   CAPE TOWN

British Library Cataloguing in Publication Data

Peyton, K. M.
 Marion's angels.
 I. Title
823'.9'1 J   PZ7.P4483   79–40676
 ISBN 0–19–271432–5

Filmset by
Northumberland Press Ltd, Gateshead, Tyne and Wear
and printed in Great Britain by
Richard Clay (The Chaucer Press) Ltd, Bungay, Suffolk.

Chapter One

Afterwards, everybody said things like, 'We might have guessed!' or, 'I don't know why it came as a surprise, not with *Marion*.' 'Well, she's always been like that, hasn't she?'

At the time it was awful, a disaster of the first order, especially for her father, although he took it more calmly than anybody. If bringing a whole orchestra to a complete standstill in the middle of a sold-out performance could actually be taken calmly by anybody, it was by him.

'It was the angels!' Marion sobbed. 'The angels—the angels flying—'

He knew what she meant, although not many would have.

'Well, that's what it's for, isn't it? The performance is for the angels, in a way. It's not the end of the world.'

He knew that they, the two of them, in spite of being the main characters in the drama, would in fact forget it very quickly, being feckless by nature (like father like daughter), but the village wouldn't forget it for a long time. They already thought Marion was cracked, and this incident wouldn't help. There were not, after all, many girls who had a church of their own—or as good as—and kept the keys and guided the tourists and cleaned up and did the flowers and directed the workmen who came occasionally in ineffectual efforts to hold it together. And not any old church at that, but a large, impressive and very beautiful fifteenth-century church built with medieval bravado on an eminence over-looking a river marsh.

'She keeps goldfish in the font,' they complained to the vicar.

'And there's a model railway set running through the choir.

It's not right.'

'No,' said the vicar. He had his own church in the village proper, two miles away, and used that. Nobody used Marion's. And to himself he added, 'God bless her. What harm does it do?'

Once the church had been the pride and glory of a busy quayside and a rich village, but the river had silted up, trade had been diverted and the village had gone with it. All that was left was a row of old cottages outside the church. Marion lived with her father in the cottage nearest to the church gate.

'If Marion didn't care for the church, who would?' the vicar gently scolded the complainers.

'But it doesn't *belong* to her,' they said.

'It belongs to God, and so does Marion.'

A typical, vicarish remark, they said, snorting and tossing their heads. But they weren't at heart unkind, only a bit shocked about the goldfish, and they all had a soft spot for Marion's father Geoff, who was only a lad himself, having married and fathered Marion in his teens. He had accepted what everyone else considered the burden of bringing up 'that queer little Marion' without recognizing it as a burden. They rubbed along together, in a necessarily unorthodox but perfectly unstrained relationship, Marion learning to cope in an adult fashion with keeping house, and herself, and shopping and cooking, and her father accepting that he was no longer free to go out with his cronies or down to the pub at night; growing up lonely, independent, but not in any way resentful. Not even growing up at all, in the opinion of many people.

'They're like two children together,' was a common remark.

Marion was quite naturally a different creature from her school friends, so aloof and capable in many ways, and yet curiously childish too, with her secret games and her strange fears. She saw ghosts; she would wake in the night, crying out about things Geoff could make head nor tail of. But he would go to her and sit on her bed and talk to her, quite matter of fact.

'He should take her to a psychiatrist,' they said at the Women's Institute, but he just sat and talked about what he would do next on his boat and if Andy came over on Sunday perhaps they might go for a row up the river as far as the bridge to see if the swans had hatched their eggs yet. Marion, wild-eyed with her nightmares, would lie with his calm chat flowing over her uncharted fears, coming back to reality.

Since his wife's death Geoff had channelled both energies and emotions into building a boat. He worked as a computer programmer by day and as a boat-builder in the evenings and at week-ends, and the life satisfied him, and Marion fitted in as well as could be expected, thank you. He had never looked for another girl-friend, and the village had given up making plans for him. A slender, gold and brown man, he had a way of not seeming to use words very much. The

3

village was fond of him and helped where it could, but he was oblivious of their concern.

He had got dragged into the concert business without much wanting to, being amiable by nature and recognizing that he was needed. The orchestra, together with a young, up-and-coming pianist, had agreed to give a concert in the church, the proceeds to go towards the roof fund. The roof, still in its original state, of timber decorated by six pairs of carved angels in the centre of the main beams, flying back to back, magnificently, was of countrywide renown, and some influential people from London had arranged the charitable evening.

'*Arranging* it is easy,' the village said with great contempt. 'What about the *work* involved?'

'It is our church,' the vicar said sharply. 'We are surely not incapable of doing the labour, given such a generous offer?'

'Church? White elephant, more like,' they said, grumbling, but not wanting to miss anything.

The Women's Institute came down and swept away Marion's jarsful of buttercups and cow-parsley and brought their homegrown delphiniums and queer blue roses in armfuls and started vying with each other in flower arrangement. Geoff, living next door, had to watch out for the arrival of the grand piano and direct it to the required spot under the lectern, and see that it was protected from any possible drips should it rain during the night. He brought his winter boat-cover up from the garden shed for the purpose, avoiding the Women's Institute as best he could.

'You'd better lock up tonight, Marion. That piano's worth three thousand quid, they say. And my cover's worth a bit too.'

'No one's going to run off with a piano,' Marion said scornfully.

4

'My cover then.'

Marion didn't like locking the church. She felt the church belonged to the land outside, and one should be free to come and go, lifting the heavy latch and passing from the great arcades of white stone inside to the tumbled hillside, lush with summer growth that fell down to the river. Her church was light inside, and high and bare, like a great barn; and the angels' wings fanned across the roof, pale and incisive in the light from the clerestory windows, just as if they were passing through, not nailed down at all, a part of the sky, drifting over the marshes like celestial herons. Marion didn't want to lock them in.

'Later,' she said, not intending to.

She got the tea, toasting some pancake things out of a packet, and unwrapping a large wedge of cheese. Her father never complained about the food.

'This concert,' she said, 'I've worked it out—it will make one thousand, eight hundred and fifty pounds for the restoration fund.'

'Less expenses,' Geoff said. 'Peanuts, considering what's wanted.'

'One hundred and fifty thousand,' Marion said.

'It's ridiculous to think—' Geoff hesitated, shrugged. 'Well, they're getting older all the time, all of them, not just ours, but Canterbury and York and Winchester and all of them, all wanting money, all the time. What do you do? Ours won't get a look in. It's too far gone. This concert will keep the rain out for another winter, that's all. A few patches.'

'You can't let it fall down.'

'Why not?'

'Because—' Because it was a part of everything that mattered, because it belonged, it had been there for five hundred years, it was the landscape.

'A whole town's gone, just down the road. What's another

church?'

'But that was the sea that took it. The sea won't touch this.'

'In a sense, it already has.'

The silting up of the river had taken the trade; the village had died, and there was no one to bother about the church. Marion knew what he meant. She knew about the town too, eaten at by the sea, the sandy cliffs eroded, the buildings falling one by one into the sea. In eleven hundred, it had been a city with walls, market places, several churches, a monastery and a harbour which did a busy trade. Now it was a scumbled beach with a few fishing boats on it, a shed where crabs were put into boxes, a car park for the nosy, and some sandy cliffs scrambling up into the woods. If you walked through the silent woods with a guide book, you could stand on a narrow track through the sycamore, grass and brambles waist-high on either side, and read: 'This is the former main street, leading from the market square to St. James's church, now three hundred yards out to sea.' Just standing there, thinking about it, Marion could feel the hair rising up on the back of her neck. She had described this phenomenon to her father, but he had just laughed.

'We used to collect bones out of the cliffs when we were kids,' he said. 'Skulls and all. Where the graveyards used to be. There's still some in the shed, I think. There's still one or two to go yet, graves, I mean, if you look along the edge. Maybe gone by now. I don't know.'

Marion, looking hard, found a stone very close to the edge, indecipherable. If it was truly a grave, it would go fairly soon, and another skeleton with it. It fascinated her.

'It might be a man who was alive in fourteen hundred. He might have helped build my church.'

'He might have, yes.'

'He might be the man that carved the angels. Swithin. He

6

carved all twelve of them, for five shillings each. They took him three years.'

'Pass the cheese.'

'He lived in that town. He walked here every day along the river, six miles, and back again at night, six miles.'

'Are you making it up?'

'No, it's true. He had nearly finished the last one when he fell off the scaffolding and broke his leg and he died sixteen days later. The angel's wing isn't finished. You can see, if you get up there.'

'When've you been up there?'

'The builders took me. I wanted to see if it was true. I asked them.'

'And you found the wing was unfinished?'

'Yes. The feathers aren't carved, like on all the others. It's just smooth.'

Geoff was quite impressed, but didn't say anything. It was a bit odd in a child, he had to admit. Liz, her mother, had studied medieval history at university and got a degree. He preferred boats himself.

'The vicar says the angels are going to have to come down fairly soon, before they come of their own accord and brain somebody.'

'Yes. The builders said. It's what the concert's for, isn't it? The roof.'

'It'll need more than a concert.'

Marion didn't lock up. She went to bed at nine o'clock and lay thinking about the money it would take to repair St. Michael's. It wasn't possible, she thought. The roof was really bad. For the concert they had had to spend two hundred pounds on a scaffolding protection beneath the most precarious of the angels, like a safety net for a trapeze act, in case it might choose that auspicious day to fall and do damage to the visitors. But the profit from the concert would

7

pay to renew their fastenings and fix them properly ... **for** the time being. Their cottage, minuscule by comparison, kept eating up money to keep in repair, and it was a mere infant compared with the church; two hundred years old as opposed to five. From her bed she could see the church through the window, framed in bird-riddled thatch. It was the anchor of her life, dominating her horizons. It was her friend, her retreat, her key to centuries past, her home.

An hour later, still awake, she heard a car go past and stop outside the church. The lane to the church was a cul-de-sac, curving down a couple of hundred yards from the main road between thick hedges. Of the people who lived in the three cottages in the lane, only her father had a car, and it wasn't his. It was a fast and snorty-sounding car, stopping sharp in a spraying of gravel. Marion got out of bed and looked out of the window. In the dusk she saw the car parked, and a figure walking across the churchyard towards the east door. Mindful of her responsibilities she got out of bed, pulled on some clothes and followed. Her father was still working on his boat down by the river at the bottom of the garden, but she didn't intend to disturb him. Church business was hers. She only had to check that the stranger had no evil intentions towards the Steinway, also her father's tarpaulin. She could wait, watching, until he drove away. People quite often drove down from the road to visit, or even to pray. It wasn't unusual. But tonight was a bit special.

She went outside, through the tangle that was their garden, across the lane and the gravelled sweep of the car park and into the churchyard. It was cool and still but the stones of the wall were warm to the touch after the day, and familiar smells, rank and rich, sifted up through the long grass from the river, through the creaming elder trees and across the mown grass. Marion walked on the grass, silently. She knew how to open the door without making a sound, to

8

push it only so far, before the squeak. She could slip in like a shadow and stand unseen, the church's keeper. But she waited outside for a while, sitting on a tombstone (Edward Tonkin, 1761–1795). No doubt the visitor was genuine and she didn't want a confrontation, being shy by nature.

She waited.

The mosquitoes were biting. She slapped at her bare legs, and flailed her arms a bit, then stopped short at an unexpected development in her vigil–the stranger was playing the piano. Above the whine of mosquitoes the notes seeped out on the still evening, spilling with undeniable skill and beauty into the immediate surroundings. Marion, knowing she should be indignant, was enchanted. It was like no piano-playing she had heard before, even from Miss Moore at school. It was real, and perfect. She stood up, but didn't want to spoil anything, so stayed where she was for quite a long time, listening. He wasn't supposed to, she was thinking, but it was much too nice to stop. She should walk in and accost him. But she knew she wouldn't.

'I will go in,' she thought, 'and listen.'

She went in, without a sound, muffling the great iron latch with her handkerchief, settling it back in its bracket, and creeping up the side aisle until she was up as far as the piano, behind a pillar, quite close to the visitor. She could see his back and his bent head, her father's tarpaulin in a heap on the floor and the lid of the piano opened, so that the playing filled the whole church, echoing and singing through the great spaces, reaching for the angels behind their bracework of scaffolding, caged like eagles, the great wings outspread. Marion could feel it taking her, could feel herself growing wings, taking off. She knew how it was with her, and tried to keep on the ground, not to get into one of her states. She crept along inside the front pew until she was past the piano and into the middle aisle, and she lay on the floor there, her head to the altar, her feet to the belltower.

'Please, God, don't let him stop.'

She could look round the corner of the pew, her head hidden by an enormous vase of flowers, and see the feet on the pedals. The legs wore jeans, she was surprised to see. Looking higher, she could see the man's face framed between the piano and the lid, pale against the white stone beyond, very grave, almost beautiful by his involvement with the music, although not beautiful in feature. It was a strong, rather fierce face, with a firm, aggressive jaw, untidy locks of hair falling forward when he bent his head towards the keys. He wore a dirty, white T-shirt with an advertisement for beer on the chest. He was quite young, younger than her father, although past being a boy. Marion stared at him through the W.I. delphiniums, in love with the creator of this lovely noise. It was better than the organ, altogether more delicate and airborne. He played without music, for love, she supposed, his expression suggesting it; yet it seemed to her very intricate music, difficult judging by the complexity of it, yet not seeming difficult. Marion held on to the coconut matting and communed with God, strung up by her experience, adrift on the tide of melody.

When it stopped, quite suddenly, she was left as if in suspension, vibrating like a wire, so alive in every fibre that it seemed impossible to stay hidden. She did not move.

The man sat still, looking at the keys for some time, then he got up, shut the lid, and heaved the tarpaulin back in place. Marion could have touched his foot with her hand. When he went round the far side to pull the cover straight, she wriggled backwards into the cover of the pew—which was as well, for he came back and stood right where her head had lain, resting his hand on the carved poppyhead. He looked towards the altar, and said, quietly but with great passion, 'Jesus, make it all work out.' He wore baseball boots with red laces and the edges of his jeans were frayed.

Then he went back to the door and let himself out, puzzled by Marion's handkerchief round the latch. He looked all round the church curiously, and examined the handkerchief, which was a babyish one with the three little pigs printed on it, then laid it carefully on the table beside the church history booklets, made some piglike snorts into the silence, added, 'Happy rootling, whoever you are,' and let himself out. In a moment Marion heard the sports car start up, turn round with some very racy accelerations, and speed off towards the main road. It disappeared into the far distance at what sounded like an illegal speed. Marion retrieved her handkerchief and let herself out. She went back to the house for the church keys, and locked the doors, and went back to bed. She lay for a long time thinking about what had happened, not curious, merely appreciative. It had been beautiful. She didn't question the pearls in her path, cast before her rootling.

*   *   *

The next afternoon, all was made plain. The orchestra arrived to rehearse, and the solo pianist arrived in his fast car: the visitor of the night before. He still wore his baseball boots and beer shirt, but was business-like and unrapt, discussing *tempi* and phrasing with the conductor, poring over the score, and playing one particular passage with the orchestra over and over again until it appeared to satisfy. Marion sat in a pew and watched and listened, enjoying this unusual bustle in her church, the chatting and scraping of chair-legs on the worn flags, laughter, the echo of a practising flute coming back from the arches of the clerestory as if a bird sat up there, mocking. They spoke of acoustics and echo, and put the brass farther back, and pushed the Steinway farther forward, and then the orchestra played something without the piano to see if the balance was right, and the pianist sat down near Marion and smoked a cigarette. Marion wanted to look at him, but daren't. He was very strongly-built, tough looking, like a bricklayer, she thought, not like a pianist at all. But he had a way of looking when he was playing that was quite different. His name was Patrick Pennington.

The vicar arrived with several of the important people in the village, Mrs. Roberts of the W.I., some of the parish councillors and old Beetle, the headmaster. The vicar said hullo to Marion, not ignoring her like most of the others, and then he went and spoke in his avuncular fashion to the pianist, who looked bored but fairly polite, and called Marion over and introduced her to him.

'This is Marion Carver, who looks after the church.'

Marion shook hands politely. The pianist's hand was large and bony and strong, but gentle, which is what she had expected. He didn't say anything, but made a noise like a pig grunting. Afterwards Marion realized that the handker-chief she had used round the latch was hanging out of her shirt pocket, showing the printed pigs, but at the time she was surprised, and so was the vicar.

'We're laying tea on for you all at the school hall,' Alfred the vicar said, recovering quickly. 'Will you come down after the rehearsal? Mr. Gibson said you'd be through by four-thirty, so you'll have an hour and a half, and the ladies will have it all ready and waiting.'

'Thank you,' Mr. Pennington said politely, but Marion got the impression that he wasn't really bothered.

She was right, for when the orchestra departed village-wards in their coach, led by the vicar in his Morris Minor, the pianist wasn't with them. He was lying stretched out on the front pew with his hands behind his head, looking at the

12

hammer-beam roof and the angels, cleverly hidden from Alfred's puzzled, departing look round.

'He's got his own car,' the conductor, Mr. Gibson, had said. 'He can find us easily enough.'

Marion went home, and told her father of the goings-on. He had come up from his boat early, fuzzed over with saw-dust, to get ready for the concert.

'You'll have to wear something nice,' he said to Marion. 'Everyone will be dressed up. Have you got anything?'

'I'll try,' Marion said. Both of them knew that this was the sort of thing they weren't very good at.

'And that pianist fellow—you should ask him over for a wash or whatever—somewhere to change, if he's on his own. I can understand him not wanting the beanfeast at the school, but he might quite like just a cup of tea in the kitchen.'

Marion got changed into a dress that her cousin in Ipswich had worn as a bridesmaid six years ago and her aunt had shortened and parcelled to Geoff; she didn't like it, but it had a best look about it, shiny and uncomfortable, which is what she thought best ought to be; then she went to look for Mr. Pennington. He was still in the front pew, looking at the roof, not asleep. He turned his head slowly as she came into his vision, and seemed to come back from somewhere far away. Marion somehow thought she knew him quite well, had known him for much longer than just since last night.

'Daddy says you can come to our house to change, if you want,' she said. 'It's just across the road.'

He sat up slowly.

'And have a cup of tea.'

'Yes,' he said.

He got up and he fetched a suitcase out of his car and followed Marion home. It was half-past five. Geoff was shaving in the kitchen mirror over the sink, and the kettle was on the boil.

'The bathroom's all yours, if you want it. Marion'll show you. And the tea will be ready when you come down.'

'Thanks.'

When he came down he looked like a completely different person, exactly like a concert pianist, in fact, in a jacket of black velvet with a pristine white shirt, an inch of cuff showing fastened with gold links, and a tie of dark red silk. His hair was very tidy, his face pale and taut. Not a bit like a bricklayer, Marion thought, blushing that it had crossed her mind. But the baseball boots ... she poured the tea, confused. And he had snorted.

'That boat by the river—is it yours? Are you building it?' he asked Geoff.

'Yes.' Geoff's face lit up.

'It's ferro?'

'Yes.'

'Who designed it?'

'Alan Hill. Do you want to have a look over her? Perhaps —if there's time—no, perhaps not—'

'Afterwards, not before. Yes, I'd like to. I'll come back after the performance. I shan't have much time though—got to play at the Pavilion at eight forty-five—that's half an hour away. It might not fit in.'

'Well, if not, another time. Or are you just here for a day or two? You travel a lot?'

'Yes, but I'm based here for the summer. I've rented a cottage on the beach. My wife's living there.'

Wife! thought Marion, stabbed. It wasn't possible! How mean! She felt crushed. Even Geoff looked slightly surprised.

'It's very kind of you to do this,' he said, turning into a good host, vicar-wise. 'For the church funds—the roof repair. It needs the money desperately.'

'For the church funds? You mean—' The questioning look turned into one of despairing resignation. 'Oh bloody hell,

I might have known. You're getting it free? Mick—my agent —said, ages ago—my fault, I'd forgotten. This is a charity do?'

Geoff was amused. 'For the work of the Lord,' he said, in Alfred's voice.

'For the good of my image, Mick said. He's no more up in the works of the Lord than I am.'

'You'll feel good afterwards.'

'I'd feel better with a cheque.'

Marion scowled at him. 'The angels need it,' she said belligerently.

'So do I,' Pennington said to her.

'They are more important.'

'Don't be rude,' said her father.

But Pennington said, 'You're probably right,' and looked gloomy. 'I'd better be off.'

'We'll come with you.'

The first cars were already arriving, and the orchestra was coming down the lane in its coach. Geoff and Marion had reserved seats in the front pew, where Marion had hidden the night before. The spikes of Mrs. Parmenter's delphiniums reached over and shed pollen over the prayer-books. Marion sneezed. She would be able to watch the pianist between the blue flowers and, since the piano had been moved forward, see his fingers twinkling over the keyboard. They must move faster than you could see, almost, she thought, remembering the music the night before. He had disappeared, presumably into the vestry to await his cue. The orchestra was going to play something else first, without him; according to the programme he was after the Siegfried Idyll by Wagner, playing a concerto by Mozart, number twenty-two in E flat. On the opposite page there was a photo of him, looking rather cross, as if remembering that he was playing for charity, and underneath it gave his life-history, all about his 'meteoric rise to acclaim' and his engagements in Europe and at the Festival Hall. It finished, 'He lives in London, is married and has a young son.' A young son! Worse and worse. Marion supposed that he had had to get married, like her own father, for getting his girl-friend pregnant. She had heard it so often, in the village, particularly at school in regard to herself, what the W.I. ladies called 'a shot-gun marriage'.... She had, and had always had, a very vivid picture in her mind of her mother and father being married, in this very church, and her grandfather Harris standing behind her father with his gun levelled between Geoff's shoulder-blades and prodding him when it came to the 'I will' part. But, the deed done, they had been very happy. Marion always remembered her mother as a very happy person. Presumably Mr. and Mrs. Pennington were too. But Marion wished he wasn't married. He was rather special, somehow.

'Have you got a handkerchief?' her father asked her, eyeing the pollen-heavy flowers.

'No.'

He found her one, and put it on the seat between them.

'You have to keep very quiet and still when they're playing. It sounds awful if people cough and sneeze.'

The church was filling up fast, the people streaming in, all in their best clothes, just about the whole village as well as the smart strangers from London and what Geoff called the 'culture-vultures' from the surrounding countryside and Alfred with the Bishop, no less, and several other ecclesiastical gentlemen who all sat in the adjoining front pew. Marion was glad about the scaffolding over their heads. Lifting her gaze, she could see the two angels she called Herbert and Ted eyeing the goings-on with obvious amazement behind the wire-netting. Swithin had done a particularly good job on that pair, for they had the faces not of angels but of village people. Marion suspected that they were real portraits, worked out of Swithin's system for fun, or affection, fixed for eternity to gaze upon the antics of twentieth-century man. No doubt their models' bones were by now swilled under by the North Sea a few miles up the coast, having spilled down the cliff like all the others—except the one. When he goes, Marion thought, soon, it will all be finished. The last physical trace of medieval man. But their angels would last for ever. Thanks to the reluctant Mr. Pennington and the orchestra from London.

The orchestra was now taking its place and the church was completely full, even people standing at the back. Marion had to keep turning round to look, never having seen it like this as far back as she could remember. It looked so strange, a different place, all humming and stirring and alive and rich, brightly-coloured, restless. Is this how it had been in the past? Is this how Swithin had seen it before he died? How could it ever have been so full, given only the local countryside to draw on, without people coming from miles in cars? It couldn't have, she decided. And yet it had been built so huge. For swank, Geoff had always said. Keeping up with the medieval Joneses. Perhaps he was right. The angels knew, if only they would speak; they had seen everything from the day their eyes had been carved. Even Swithin's face bending over them. Marion had gone into one of her trances and didn't stand up when the vicar gave his address and asked the Bishop to lead them in a blessing before the performance. Her father hauled her to her feet and she came to just in time for the amen, and sat down again with everyone else. The orchestra got settled, turning up the corners of their music, and the conductor raised his baton. A deep, expectant silence filled the church. The evening sun streamed in through the windows and the conductor couldn't see his woodwind, squinting into the light.

Geoff had always said about music, 'It's not so much

listening to it, as the thoughts you think while it's playing.'
Perhaps the Siegfried Idyll made him think about sailing on
a summer sea, for it fitted, and he looked perfectly happy, in
spite of having had to come in from his boat early and put
a suit on. Marion went back to her angels, and Swithin, and
kept an eye on Herbert and Ted in case the vibrations might
dislodge them; but the music was gentle, not the dislodging
kind. Above the choir, Sebastian and Arthur, the most angelic
of the twelve, very pure of feature, bland and not as like-
able as the others, stretched out their time-bleached wings
and hung above the serenade as if aware that it was all for
them, aloof and lovely, ungrateful. But Herbert and Ted
quivered behind the wire-netting, amazed, peering nosily.
The clapping at the end of the piece startled them as much
as it startled Marion. She was watching them, saw them
vibrate to the noise, winced.

'Come back, come back,' her father said gently. 'Did you
like it?'

'Yes.'

'It's our Mr. Pennington now.'

'It's lovely. I didn't think it would be like this.'

'No. It's a perfect setting for such music.'

The conductor was returning, followed by Pennington,
who winkled his way to the Steinway round the delphiniums
and bowed briefly to the applause. He looked very distant
and unsmiling. He sat down at the piano and fidgeted himself
into the right position, brushed some pollen off his sleeve and
then sat still, his hands resting on his thighs. The conductor
looked at him and he nodded. The conductor lifted up his
baton and the instruments, all in position, hung on his word,
then burst into action with a chord that made Marion jump,
then, instantly, a cheerful tune and some quite joky bits with
a bassoon, so that Marion was charmed. It was so long before
the pianist came in that she had quite forgotten about him,

sitting motionless behind the delphiniums. Then, suddenly, he lifted up his hands and the tune was all his, not grandiose at all, but very simple and delicate, so delicate that she remembered, blushing ... bricklayer ... how could she? Yet he was very strong, almost aggressive looking, not thin and poetic at all; he was how she had imagined Swithin might have looked, even to the hands being so strong and big and yet so meticulous ... she watched them, steeped in her thoughts, and his face too, looking as Swithin's must have done at work on his carving—wrapt and intense with concentration, the features transformed by the will to create something of rare beauty, of great difficulty; a craftsman's face expressing the mixed pain and joy of delivering the finished work ... she had never guessed at it before, but now it was before her very eyes, all bound up with Swithin and the angels. It was what her father had said, not exactly the music but what it provoked in one's head. It lifted her up in the strangest way. She felt dangerously moved, knew the feeling, loved it, knew its dangers, but did not want to know. She looked up at the angels and saw them moving, great wings outstretched, their faces shining. It was very hot. They wanted to fly, straining at their tender restraints, their wing-tips pulsating ... Ted and Herbert bursting at the wire-netting. She could see them moving. She stood up. It was terribly hot. The music was filling the whole roof with a great pulsating, unleashing the angels from their centuries of silent immobility. In a moment the roof would split open and they would take off like great white barn owls, borne on a tide of celestial music. She knew it was going to happen.

'No!' she shouted at them. 'Don't go! You mustn't go!'

She made a great convulsive leap out of the pew and ran. But the enormous pot of delphiniums was right in her path and she kicked it over with a crash. A deluge of water gushed out into Pennington's lap, the delphiniums toppling like pine-trees in clouds of bright pollen. The conductor dropped his baton. Geoff was out of his pew in a flash and made a dive for Marion, wrapping his arms tightly round her on the stone flags, scooping her up.

'Idiot!' he hissed in her ear. 'Little idiot!' and ran, holding her in his arms, right down the aisle and out of the door; leaving behind a stunned silence which was broken only by the amazed dying away of various instruments, cacophonous with shock.

Pennington disentangled himself from the delphiniums, pushing them all on the floor. His shoes were full of water.

The conductor crossed over to him, white-faced.

'Jesus, Pat! What was all that about?'

'I'm sorry,' Pennington said. 'Couldn't help stopping—a physical impossibility to continue, for delphiniums. But now, if you like, the beginning of the movement.'

'You're soaking wet.'

'Please, let's go on. Talk about it later.'

'If you like.'

The conductor went back to his rostrum; muttered to the strings, and raised his baton. The fluttering, twittering audience fell silent, a patter of spasmodic applause broke out, and the music started again. Pennington leaned his arms on the top of the piano, his hands over his face, waiting. Then, when it was nearly time for him to come in, he shifted back into position, rubbed his palms down his thighs, dried the dampness off on the flanks of his velvet jacket, and started to play. As if nothing had happened.

*   *   *

'You're all right now, idiot child?'

Geoff dropped a gentle hand from around Marion's shoulders and sat back from her, regarding her with concern. They were sitting on a tombstone (William and Maria, his wife, Peterson, 1820–1858 and 1817–1890) at the bottom of the churchyard, alone, and Marion, having sobbed hysterically into the front of Geoff's best suit for nearly ten minutes, was beginning to recover.

'I'm sorry! I'm sorry!'

'Sorry for what? Worse things happen at sea.'

'I didn't mean—'

'No. Don't think about it.'

'They'll say—'

He smiled, dabbing at his wet suit with a handkerchief. 'Who's worrying? I'll make the apologies, say all the right things to the right people. You'll grow out of it.'

'Do you think?'

'I do. Like catarrh and adenoids and things.'

Marion sniffed.

'Mind you,' Geoff added, glancing at his watch, 'I think it might be politic to disappear until everyone's gone home. I'll go up and have a word with Alfred tonight, later. We can write a note to the Bishop and the conductor.'

'And the pianist.'

'Yes, poor boy. I have a feeling we might see him again, about the boat. He probably won't hold it against you.'

Marion wasn't so sure, remembering the intense involvement that had—partly—set her off, getting him mixed up with Swithin and the angels. She had a deep, painful guilt feeling towards the pianist. He had been nice. Her sort of person. Not a bit as stuffy as she thought professional pianists ought to be.

Geoff said, 'I think I'll change and go back on the boat, do a bit of work. I don't fancy showing my face here for a bit. Want to come?'

'I'll stay here, where no one can see me. Just lie in the grass.'

'You're sure it's O.K. now? All quiet on the western

front?' That was one of his expressions, an old book title, which he used for such times. Marion smiled.

'Yes.'

'You know where I am then. Don't brood about it.'

'No.'

That was nice about Geoff, that he didn't fuss, Marion thought, after he had gone away. Always there if you wanted, but aware of a person's need for being alone. He was a lonely person too, but happy with it. How awful if he had listened to those busybody women saying she needed treatment ... if *he* had said she was ... well, how did they describe it? 'Disturbed' ... was the word they used. Flint, the boy at the Post Office, the nearest she had to a best friend, called it 'mad' in the old-fashioned way, perfectly cheerful about it ... 'my mad friend Marion,' he said ... but her father said it was the working of an over-active imagination. She wasn't sure what that meant, but it sounded as if

one might conceivably be proud of it. He said she would grow
out of it, or learn to cope. 'Nothing to *worry* about,' he said
to her. So she didn't. Only sometimes, like now, it was a
bit of an embarrassment, and she felt really bad about the
pianist.

She went to the bottom of the churchyard and lay behind
a mossy tomb, an elder tree making a cave from the strong
evening sunlight. The sun was low and very warm, the
shadows long. A moorhen was making noises below her, on
the mud. The smell of grass cuttings rose heavily from the
compost heap behind the wall: all very familiar and homely
and comforting. The church was like a great white ship in her
vision, breasting her horizon, a vast mother hen to the tombstone chicks. It matters more than all the other things,
Marion thought.

Presumably the interval had arrived, for a great many of
the audience came out into the churchyard and started walk-

ing about and standing in small groups talking. Some of them came down to look at the river, and stood quite close to where Marion lay. She knew they wouldn't see her. She was curled in the nest of the elder tree, her cheek against lichened stone, invisible. She could see spiky-heeled patent-leather shoes pecking into the turf like a green woodpecker's beak, fat nylon legs. . . .

'What an embarrassment for her poor father! Although, naturally, I blame him—letting her run wild the way he does. She's like a little scarecrow—'

'Well, it's in the blood. Her mother was none too stable, as I remember.'

Marion thought of Liz as non-too-stable. She saw the word all run into one: nontoostable. They were a nontoostable family. The woman meant it in a derogatory sense but Marion, seeing the word like that, thought it was a nice word; they had been a nice family, the three of them, happy and hard-working and careless; Marion would rather have had a mother like Liz for seven years, than one like fat-nylon-legs for ever.

After a while they all dribbled back into the church. Marion lay watching, her chin propped on her hands. The east door opened suddenly, and a figure came out alone. Everyone else was back in, the churchyard silent and golden in the last of the sun. The figure came slowly down towards the river, picked one of the more comfortable tombstones with its slab nicely warmed by the setting sun, and sat down on the grass, leaning back wearily. It was the pianist. Marion, trapped in her hiding-place, watched him with a worried expression. She felt very bad about the pianist. It struck her that God was presenting her with the opportunity to apologize. But the thought of it made her heart thump uncomfortably. He looked formidable in his concert clothes, his face very grim, his attitude dejected. She realized that she was spying on him,

24

which made it worse. He thought he was alone but she could watch his every movement. It was the awful, guilty embarrassment of her situation that spurred her to get up and drag herself reluctantly across the grass to where he sat. Her throat was too tight to let any words out. She stood with her head down, not wanting to look.

She heard him give a grunt of recognition.

'What was it about my playing that made you scream and run? Tell me.'

She could not answer.

He wasn't smiling. He was chewing a piece of grass, scowling. He didn't look like the same person who had been playing the Mozart, like Swithin carving the angels. More like Swithin having a row with his wife. How to explain?

'It was because . . .' Impossible. 'The angels—' Geoff had understood. He always did. But Mr. Pennington was a stranger.

And yet, daring to look at him again, Marion had this odd feeling once more that she knew him very well, had known him all her life. There was something about him which stirred a core in her bones, way back. Something to do with her over-active imagination? A feeling, a cobweb, groping . . . how could it be?

'I was watching the angels in the roof, and the music was so beautiful that I thought they were real, and they started to fly, and I thought the roof would open up and they would fly away, and I couldn't bear it, so I shouted, "No!"'

He looked up at her, taking the grass out of his mouth. His eyes, under drawn-down brows, were very sharp, rather frightening.

'It's true,' she said. 'You might not believe me, but it's true.'

'I believe you,' he said.

He put the grass back and sighed.

25

'It wasn't nice for me, but—perhaps—a compliment of a sort.'

'I'm sorry.'

'Don't be.'

She sat down on the grass beside him, relieved by his understanding.

'That concert, you see, it was for the roof, and the angels first—you know that—to fix them so that they won't fall. Perhaps I was thinking that, thinking about them falling, and it made me see them flying. I was thinking about the man who made them, and watching you and your expression was like the man's when he carved the angels.'

Pennington turned his head and looked at her again, curiously. From experience Marion knew that most people laughed at her if she what they called 'carried on in that way', but he didn't laugh.

'I looked at those angels for a long time,' he said, 'after the rehearsal, and I felt they could well fly away.'

Marion remembered him lying in the pew when everyone else went to the W.I. tea, hands behind his head.

'It was the music,' she said.

'You don't want to get seats for the Festival Hall then. Not without your daddy there to field you.'

'I'm sorry.'

They sat for a long time in silence. They were in the last of the sun which came slanting sideways between a gap in the elms and the alder. The trees fringed the churchyard before the land fell away down banks of nettles and meadow-sweet to the river. Beyond the river the cows were grazing on golden pasture, casting long thin shadows. The road was quiet.

Eventually Pennington sighed and said, 'It's nice here. Makes you think.'

'What about?'

'Things you don't have time to think about usually. Some-one carving those angels, for instance.'

'Swithin,' Marion said.

'Was that his name?'

'It's in the records. Fourteen twenty to fourteen fifty-three. He died of a broken leg.'

'What a waste.'

'But he did that first. It's more important, doing that, and dying at thirty-three, than dying at seventy having done nothing.'

'I agree.'

'I thought, when you were playing, that he could have been a bit like you. I imagine him like you. The way you look when you play.'

'How do I look when I play?'

'Beautiful. But when you're not playing you're just ordinary.'

The sharp, ordinary eyes looked at her with a suggestion of astonishment.

'Do people ever tell you you're mad?'

'No. "Disturbed", they say.'

'Yes, of course. They said that about me once.'

'*Did* they?' Marion was enchanted.

'Disturbed. Aggressively motivated. Emotionally deprived. All the jargon.'

'Really? Why? What did you do?'

'I used to hit people if they annoyed me.'

'Badly? I mean, hard?'

'Hard enough to get me locked up. "Grievous bodily harm" it's called.'

'Locked up? You mean in prison?'

'Yes.'

'*Really?*' Marion was enormously impressed.

'Twice.'

27

'Do you do it now?'

'No. I've grown out of it.'

'Daddy says I'll grow out of it.'

'Yes, it's the same thing. Feelings you can't control. But I dare say you won't go to prison for yours.'

'A mental home.'

'Perhaps. But it doesn't seem that bad to me. What you did, in the church, is ... to me ... more natural, if the music is good enough, than—well ... some people read their programmes, or go to sleep.'

'Truly?'

'Yes. I've seen them.'

'You don't mind about me then?'

'Well, it's perhaps a rather inconvenient way to react, stopping us all in our tracks. But what I'm saying is that I understand. Some might not.'

'No. It's going to be awful—the church ladies will say things. Alfred—the vicar—he might be a bit cross too.'

'Tell them, from me, that it's all right.'

'Thank you, I will.'

'I'd better go. I've got to go and play Chopin in the Festival Pavilion. And call home for some dry trousers first.'

'Truly, I'm sorry.'

He smiled, for the first time. He had an essentially serious expression, and did not smile often.

'It was an interesting evening. Thank you. I'll come and call on you soon to see your father's boat, if he won't mind.'

'No. He loves showing people his boat.'

They got up and walked down the path to the lane where the green sports car was parked. Pennington got in and started the engine.

'Good-bye, little idiot.'

'Thank you,' Marion said.

Chapter Two

Mr. Pennington came round to the cottage four days later, in the evening, to look at Geoff's boat. Geoff was working on it, and Marion was sitting on a saw-bench, having brought him a cup of tea. The back garden was long and narrow, neglected since Liz had died, and overgrown with old roses and mint and golden rod. It sloped quite steeply down to the river and petered out at the bottom into salty grass and sea-lavender, for the river was tidal and the banks were seamed with mud-channels. At low tide there was no river, only mud-banks. But at high-water springs the river came right up over the saltings and lipped at the golden rod, and sent scummy fingers up the garden path as if it would explore the back kitchen, given encouragement.

Geoff's boat stood just clear of the high water mark, propped up with old sleepers, a sleek grey hull which Marion always thought looked like a sea-lion hoping for titbits. The metal-framed hull had already been plastered and the deck was on, and Geoff was doing the inside joinery. So far it had taken him two years. He didn't think about very much else. He had a friend in the village called Horry who helped him quite often, steaming and laminating and bolting through and offering up ... Marion took it as a way of life, and couldn't foresee the day when the boat might be launched.

When Pennington arrived to have a look, Marion took him down the garden and left them talking about four layers of half-inch mesh, to make a five-eighths shell—much in the same way, she thought, as the musicians had talked about the *rallentando* leading to the second subject with a modulation into the minor key ... everything could be given a name

and place, if you *knew*, she thought, save in her own cloudy
world of feelings and intuitions ... she would learn, she
supposed, given time. She wanted to talk some more with
Pennington, but not particularly about boats. Perhaps he
would come back to the house afterwards, for a cup of tea.
But it didn't get dark till about ten. The evenings were long
and warm and still. Marion went across the lane towards
the church, wondering if Flint would come up to play with
the trains. They had made a new siding into the choir stalls,

but hadn't tried it out yet. She went into the churchyard, and saw a woman she didn't know sitting on the grass looking out across the valley. She had a child with her of about three or four, who was digging a hole in the gravel chippings on the old vicar's grave with a piece of stick. As the vicar had had eleven children of his own, Marion didn't think he would mind. She knew the couple were Pennington's wife and son and stopped to consider them, intensely curious.

The wife was only a girl; if she was even as old as twenty, Marion thought, she didn't look it. She was thin, dark, with a very grave, gentle face. She was dressed in a long flowery cotton skirt and a thin white shirt, sleeves rolled up to show brown, bony elbows, a plain gold bracelet on one wrist. For the first time in two or three years, Marion was reminded very vividly, painfully, of her own mother. It wasn't

31

particularly the looks, but something in the manner that touched an extremely vulnerable chord: the seriousness, perhaps, of someone absorbing a landscape, the sense of someone actively enjoying the summer-evening tranquility, the body in complete repose yet the spirit aware, alight. Marion could remember this in her mother, sitting on the sand-dunes watching the sea sometimes, while she had played, or wandering round a village churchyard to garner something for her sheaves of notes. It came back with a quite dreadful, sudden sense of loss. She stopped and stared, knowing it was rude, as bad almost as busting up the concert, but unable—as then—to do the right thing; hardly able, in fact, to keep from bursting into tears.

The girl looked up and stared back.

Marion, trying desperately hard, said, 'Are you Mrs. Pennington?' Her voice sounded very queer.

'Yes. Ruth. Are you Marion?'

'Yes.'

She smiled. 'I've heard about you.'

'Oh. Yes.' Marion could guess. She felt her cheeks going bright red. But embarrassment was far better than grief. It was almost a relief.

'Awful—' she muttered. 'I—' What to be said? Nothing. She stopped trying. Looked at her feet. Why was she so bad at everything?

Ruth said, 'He told me, about the angels wanting to burst out. I've been looking at them. I can imagine ... I think it was a great compliment to the players, that they moved you so much.'

'He—sort of—said that.' But only Geoff knew with what fatal ease it happened.

'It's much better, for him, than your falling asleep.'

'Yes. He said.'

'Good. He said the right things. Sometimes he's rather

32

rude.'

'Oh.' Like her. She was in good company.

'You've looked in the church?'

'Yes. I would have stayed, but Lud likes the graves best. He's not doing any harm, I don't think—' She checked up, turning to regard the oblivious child burrowing like a terrier —'The angels are fantastic. I've never seen any like that before.'

'No. There aren't any.'

'What's their history? When was the church built?'

Marion, encouraged and grateful, told her the story of the great church's ambitious beginning, lording it over the surrounding countryside with the ships coming in and out to load at its feet and the big road winding inland to connect up with market towns and villages all the way to London.

'Until the marshes started to silt up and big storms altered the river mouth so that the ships couldn't use it, and it all started to go into a decline. You can still see the remains of the old quays. There's one at the bottom of our garden, where Daddy's building the boat.'

'So the poor church has been virtually unused for centuries, not just the last few years . . . that's why it's so far gone.'

'Yes. It's been used for a barn sometimes.'

'It's all ghosts, this part,' Ruth said. 'Up the coast there, where the whole town has fallen in the sea, and this . . . it's very creepy. There's a grave, right on the edge of the cliff—'

'I know. It will go this winter, Daddy says. It's very old. Have you looked at it?'

'Yes.'

'It's fifteenth century. It used to be in the north-west corner of the churchyard of St. James. The church went in eighteen eighty something. Then all the rest of the churchyard, right to the wall. Daddy said you could pick up bones

33

all over the place after a big storm. He's got some in the shed.'

'And just one left . . . I wonder who he was? When he goes. . . .'

Marion had never had a more absorbed audience. Ruth's face was stark, thinking about it. Marion said, very tentatively: 'Sometimes—that grave—I think it might—it just *might*—be the grave—of—' She stared at the grass very intently, a little afraid of revealing her painful theory. 'It might be the man who carved the angels.'

'Why? Do people say it's his grave? Do they know?'

'No. I've never heard anyone else say. But he died in fourteen fifty-three, and he was buried in the north-west corner of the graveyard.'

'How do you know?'

'My mother knew. It's all in her notes. She studied it for her thesis. She knew an old man who said. He had notes too, masses of them. But he died and his wife burned them all, and my mother cried. Then she died. But I've still got her notes.'

'All about the church?'

'Mostly. The man who carved the angels was called Swithin. He was quite famous in his day. He did work for other churches, but I've never seen any. It might not still be there. In my mother's notes it says, 'He lived for his werke, and took no wyf.' When you get to know the angels very well, you think—a bit—you think you—almost—know him.'

She had never said this to anyone else, not even her father.

'I was thinking that, in the concert. It made me think, watching Mr. Pennington when he was playing, that it was —perhaps—the same thing, in a sort of way . . . the way he looked, playing—it made me think it was like Swithin carving the angels, how he would have looked . . . both of them,

34

making something very beautiful—it made me think of Swithin—I thought—' But it was beyond her, to put in words the wraiths and confusions in her mind. Strangely, with Ruth, these confessions did not embarrass her. There was nobody else she would have spoken to in this way, not even her father. Ruth, like her husband, was special. She could not say how. Like her husband, she accepted what Marion was saying without amusement, without patronage. Her face was understanding.

'I know what you mean.'

'He has a face like a workman, not an artist, but when he plays it looks quite different. And I thought that is how Swithin is—was. It fitted exactly. It was like them—being —the same person. I thought it was like watching Swithin.'

Ruth didn't say anything, and they both sat in silence, watching the child digging. Marion had no more to say, slightly exhausted by the effort of making articulate her difficult feelings but—somehow—lightened in a curious way by having done so. Or, perhaps, by not having been ridiculed. Perhaps she wasn't as mad as they thought. Ruth evidently didn't think so, for after an interval she said again, 'I know what you mean.' And then, 'He lives for his work too, and whether he needs a wife or not I sometimes wonder.'

This was deeper water than Marion could cope with, but the words were calmly spoken, not bitter. Perhaps, Marion thought, it could be as difficult actually having somebody as not having anybody at all.

They sat in silence for a few minutes, perfectly companionable, and then Marion, remembering her manners, said, 'Would you like to come home and have a cup of tea?'

'That would be very nice,' Ruth said.

They put the grave back tidily, and Ruth took Lud's hand and they went back to the cottage. Lud was a doer, and started to fill one of Geoff's gumboots with potatoes out of

35

a paper sack by the kitchen door, which seemed to both Ruth and Marion a reasonable way to spend the time. Marion put the kettle on and said, 'Do sit down. I'll make one for Daddy and Mr. Pennington as well.'

'He's called Pat,' Ruth said. 'Not Mr. Pennington.'

'Does he want to build a boat?'

'No. He'd never have the time. But he likes sailing. He used to sail. It would be good for him to have something apart from music, for a relaxation.'

'Isn't music a relaxation?'

Ruth laughed. 'No. Not if you're a professional.'

Marion was puzzled. 'But he only plays concerts sometimes. Not every night?'

'He plays two or three a week.'

'He has lots of spare time then?'

'No. All the rest of the time he's either travelling, or practising.'

'Practising?' Marion didn't think he needed it.

'Yes. All the time he's at home. Now we're here, he comes on the beach for an hour, has a swim perhaps. That's not much time off.'

Marion had imagined a very carefree life, sight-seeing in the fast car, sun-bathing, playing with Lud, tossing off the occasional concert. She had assumed he wanted to build a boat to fill in all his spare time. She had to readjust. There was more to piano playing than she had thought.

'I thought it was something he could just do—a gift.'

Ruth smiled. 'He can only do it so well because he has spent so much time learning how.'

It was fairly obvious when pointed out, and Marion felt ashamed. She blushed.

Ruth said, 'Nearly everybody thinks the same. Even people like my mother. It's only when you live with it, you see how it is. I didn't know, before I met him. He told me he was studying zoology. He said afterwards I would have thought he was just a layabout if he'd said music.'

'Zoology?'

Ruth laughed. 'It was a misunderstanding. I was very dim. He let me think it. Sometimes now I wish it was true.'

'Why?'

'He's away so much. And when he's home he works all the time. And I can't join in, I can't even talk music very much. His agent, Mick, comes over and they talk—they talk about a European tour, and an American one. They are dying to go to America. If they go to America. . . .' She sighed.

'Wouldn't you like to go to America?'

'Not like that. Living in hotels, travelling with Lud, waiting, meeting all those people I can't talk to.'

Ruth stopped and looked at Marion curiously. 'I don't know why I am saying this to you. I've never said it to anybody before. I wouldn't say it to anyone else.'

Marion thought, I said all that to her too, in the churchyard, which I wouldn't have said to anyone else.

Ruth said, 'I suppose it follows on, from what you said about Swithin, living for his work.' She smiled. 'It doesn't matter.'

It did, Marion knew.

'The tea's ready,' she said. 'I'll give Daddy a shout.'

Geoff came up the garden with Pat and they came in, the kitchen darkening to their figures in the doorway. Geoff was surprised by Ruth, stopping abruptly when he saw her sitting at the table. Marion, watching him, wondered if he saw in her what she had seen, the remembrance of Liz. She could not tell. Her father didn't reveal very much, as a rule. Ruth got up and they shook hands. The little kitchen seemed very full, and the mugs were all chipped, Marion noticed. She poured the milk in a jug, but the sugar in the sugarbowl was all lumpy and stuck to the sides. The teapot had a rubber spout, after she had dropped it. It wasn't very smart. Nobody seemed to notice.

'You're staying here for the summer?' Geoff said to Ruth. 'You've got a cottage at Oldbridge, Pat tells me.'

'Yes, almost on the beach. It's lovely. You must come over, with Marion.'

'It's a right old beehive, Oldbridge, at Festival time,' Geoff said. 'All those music buffs. When does the Festival start? On Saturday?'

'Yes.'

'That's why you're here? To play?'

'I've got three concerts,' Pat said.

'In the Festival Hall?' Marion asked, awed.

'Yes.'

Marion was impressed by such stature. 'Can I—we—come? I'd *love* to—'

'God forbid!' Pat said. 'I'll have you locked out.'

Geoff laughed.

'Oh, I wouldn't—I promise! Not in the hall. I wouldn't.'

'No guarantee,' Geoff said. 'You know it isn't.'

'Truly—'

'Absolutely no.'

Pat, seeing her face, said, 'Come over to the cottage and I'll play you a private concert, all to yourself, and you can scream and jump about to your heart's delight, and I promise I won't stop. I'll go right on to the end, regardless.'

'Really? Would you?'

'If you'd like it.'

'You could both come over to supper one evening,' Ruth said. 'After the Festival would be best though. Pat will be nicer then.'

'Isn't he now?' Marion asked dubiously.

'Not very.'

Pat did not disagree, stirring sugar into his tea. Perhaps

to change the subject, he said, 'How are the angels? Going to get a refit with all that lovely money?'

'The Church Commissioners are sending an inspector next week,' Geoff said. 'To examine the fabric, they say. Estimate costs. I can't see it being on, myself. Its day is over.'

Marion could not bear to hear her father talk like this.

'They will fix the angels, surely? And the roof? That wouldn't be terribly expensive.'

'The roof would. Before long it's only going to need a real gale—the tower is suspect. I think they might have to close it.'

'I would still go in,' Marion said.

'Yes, and I wish you wouldn't,' her father said. 'But I reckon anyone'd have a job to keep you out of where you want to go.'

'They *can't*,' Marion said, agonized by the thought.

Her father said, gently, 'You can't shut your eyes to it, Marion. They can't just let it fall down on a posse of unsuspecting tourists. Very bad for the reputation. Not to mention the tourists.'

Having lived with the possibility so long, Marion couldn't face the thought of the church being shuttered up, demolished. If the inspectors were coming next week, it would be decided quite soon, one way or the other.

'Don't think about it,' Ruth said gently. 'The things you worry about most, often never happen.'

'Don't they?' said Pat.

'Oh, you're different. You chose it that way.'

When they had gone, her father went down to the boat and tidied up and came back to the kitchen. Marion made some cheese sandwiches—they had had their tea earlier—and Geoff fetched a can of beer from the dresser. It was going dark. They sat by the empty fireplace. The back door was still open, and a few bats whirled about in the square of darkening sky, and the smell of roses came with the evening

39

dew.

Geoff said, 'That girl, Ruth—she reminds me—' He stopped.

Marion waited, but he didn't say any more, only, 'Your bedtime, tiddly-wink.'

Marion brushed the crumbs off the plates and put them away. She went to the staircase that led out of the kitchen.

'She reminded me, too,' she said. And went upstairs.

Chapter Three

The examination of the church structure took place a few days later, with much coming and going and measuring and chin-stroking, gouging and scraping and hammering and muttering. Marion, mostly at school, watched as best she could, and spent a lot of time polishing the brass and doing the flowers and pretending she wasn't interested if they were still there when she came home. On the third day they got Colin Pewsey the local builder in, with his ladders and a bit more scaffolding, and Marion was able to inquire of him. He had been in the same class as Geoff at school.

'Well, it's all possible, if the money's available,' he reported. 'It's the roof timbers, mainly. The beetle's got in 'em. They need replacing, and you don't find those sort of timbers so easy these days. The rest of it—well, it's deteriorating, but it's not dangerous, apart from the tower. The top of the tower's bad. That'd best be taken down, then there'd be no worries when the wind blows hard. It's all possible if they can produce the money. But my guess is, they won't. They'll make an estimate for making it safe, like, and it'll be too hefty to raise, and they'll board it all up.'

Alfred came down later and confirmed Colin's guess.

'They say a quarter of a million, just for the roof. I think they expect to make some sort of an appeal, but not with any hope of getting enough. It's a very sad position, but it doesn't come as a surprise.'

'And if they don't get it—?'

'Well, who knows? If it's not repaired they will have to stop people entering, for their own safety, and I suppose the tower will have to come down if it's dangerous, and then ...'

he glanced at Marion, somewhat anxiously. 'But what does a church matter to a child like you? It's not right to care so much, Marion. It's not—' He paused. He was going to say 'natural', but let the phrase die. 'You will get used to the idea. It's in the nature of things. Nothing material lasts for ever. Can you not accept it?'

'I couldn't watch, if they knock it down.' Her face was as white as chalk. 'What about the angels?' she asked.

'The angels, strangely, are in remarkably fine condition. Only their fastenings need replacing.'

'What will happen to them if the church is closed?'

'I expect they will go to a museum.'

'But they need—'

Marion couldn't say it. They needed space, they needed the great barn of St. Michael's about them and the sky through the unstained clerestory windows and the seagulls outside, as they were used to. A dusty museum, with neon lighting, and grubby school-parties staring into Sebastian's heavenly, far-fixed eyes; it just wasn't something she could accept.

'There's nothing wrong in what's happening, Marion. Only sad. Think how many of our treasures never survived the Reformation.'

Marion didn't know what he was talking about. It was just that she belonged to St. Michael's, and St. Michael's to her, by virtue of having been born by its gates and lived with its angels and her mother's love for it ever since she could remember. Whatever Alfred had to say, nothing could reconcile her to the thought of looking out of the window and there being no church there. It was in the same vein as a sea drying up or a mountain falling through the ground. It had never been, until now, a possibility.

'Not to—knock it down,' she said bleakly.

To decay, moulder, crumble, over another century or so . . .

42

perhaps; even to be snatched into a rampaging sea like St. James, but to be *demolished* . . . she had seen them, in Ipswich once, bludgeoning defenceless cottages with empty windows, like blind eyes, young men with bulldozers, rolling cigarettes between-times and reading the *Sun* with their sandwiches in their lunch-hour. The tears welled up.

Alfred said briskly: 'You must be sensible, girl. What if the roof fell on you and killed you? The Church is reponsible for the safety of its congregations. It is something you will have to accept. You will get used to the idea.'

'It would not kill *me*,' she said, certain.

Colin had left his ladders and scaffolding, and she went in when home to lunch and climbed up into the roof and on to the walkway. She knew it was strictly forbidden by everybody, but she had done it before, and knew no one would come in until Colin came back. It was very high and very impressive and slightly breathtaking, not because of the height, but because of being actually face to face with Herbert and Ted, close enough to see Swithin's chisel marks and the incised patterns, very formal, on their outstretched wings, and the lines on their sardonic faces. She could stroke the wood, as Swithin must have stroked it. She found it very moving.

There was nothing medieval in the faces; they were village people, as there were village people now, the same: the cautious, slightly sceptical expression of the middle-aged countryman. The other pairs of angels were less earthy, mostly quite a lot more angelic-looking, culminating in the very pious pair over the altar, Sebastian and Arthur. Marion's guess was that Swithin had started with them, and made them according to the book, proper churchy angels, but as he had progressed he had got more and more interested in carving faces of character—knowing, after all, that nobody in the congregation was ever going to come close enough

43

to recognize their grandfather or mother-in-law in his portraits; he was pretty safe, some seventy feet up, to indulge his acute perception of character. After Sebastian and Arthur there were two rather pretty youths, Humphrey and Percy, in the angelic mould but with rather more than a suspicion of spotty adolescence about them, in the pouting underlip

and roving eye; Tom and Jed, a devil-may-care couple, very
happy-looking, were followed by two old cross-patches, the
Sourapples; and the Farmer pair, a touch cross-eyed, squinted
towards the windows over the river as if looking for rain-
clouds. Marion's favourite pair were Herbert and Ted, with
their lively, watchful eyes, firmly on the congregation below.
Picking out the fidgets, Marion thought. She touched the
smooth, rounded serpentines of their twisting locks, leaving
fingermarks in the thin dust.

She could see the church as they saw it from the rafters,
very austere and empty ... neglected ... 'Useless,' she
thought, almost out loud. Alfred said that early on, before the
Reformation (whatever that was) the church had had dark,
coloured windows and had been very ornate, with a painted
rood-screen and painted walls, and a gilded canopy over the
altar, covered with carvings and statues. 'It would have
been dark and mysterious, with candles burning, and full of
the smell of incense.' How very peculiar, Marion thought,
looking down on its paleness, the clear, white stone pillars,
the bleached pinkish flagstones. Herbert and Ted had seen
all manner of changes. Another wouldn't hurt them, perhaps.
They had been around sixty times longer than she had, and

45

knew a whole lot of things she didn't know.

A figure had been decided by the end of the week, the figure that would enable the church to stay open without endangering its visitors.

Colin told her what it was.

'Seven hundred and fifty thousand pounds. That's three quarters of a million.'

It sounded a lot, somehow.

Geoff agreed. 'Crazy. You could build a hospital for that. Well—you could have, once. It's a terrible lot of money. For nothing.'

'No. Not for nothing.'

'A matter of opinion.'

Patrick agreed too. Marion met him in the church, by chance, just after dinner on Sunday. She had gone across with a bunch of slightly caterpillar-riddled roses to put on the altar, to show that somebody cared, and as she passed up the aisle a voice from the front pew startled her.

'Hi.'

He was lying stretched out on his back, his hands linked behind his head. He looked extremely smart and for a moment she didn't recognize him. She stopped and studied him, and a wide smile of pleasure spread across her face. 'It's you,' she said stupidly.

He sat up, in no great hurry, and glanced at his watch.

'Are you going somewhere?' Marion asked.

'You could say that, yes. Shortly.'

'Where?'

'To the Festival Hall.'

'Oh! It's today? This afternoon! Your concert?'

'Yes.'

'Oh, how I wish I could come!'

He grinned. 'How glad I am you're not.'

In spite of the smile he looked rather miserable and pale,

even slightly greenish.

'Why are you here? Did you want to see Daddy?'

'No.'

He paused, but saw that she needed an answer.

'I just like to come somewhere quiet, before anything—that—that matters—matters a lot, that is, and this is a nice place. On the way, you see.'

'Oh.'

He glanced at his watch again. 'I'd better go.'

'Does it matter a lot this afternoon?'

'Yes.'

'Did it when you played here?'

'No. Not like it matters today.'

She felt very relieved by his assurance. She started to walk back down the aisle with him.

He said, 'What did they find out, those surveyor chappies? Did they come and look at the roof?'

'Seven hundred and fifty thousand pounds, they said. To make it safe.'

Pat whistled. 'That's quite a few concerts.'

'Daddy says impossible.'

'Nothing's impossible—speaking from experience. Unlikely, perhaps. What you want is a rich American. Or an Arab sheikh. Pray for one—you've all afternoon.'

She looked at his face but it was quite serious.

'I wouldn't like it to go either,' he said.

'Daddy said it needs a miracle.'

'Well, I believe in miracles.'

'Truly?'

'Yes. They happen.'

Marion was doubtful. 'I'll try,'—they reached his car, and he got in—'I'll go and pray for a rich American.'

'Put one in for me too,' he said.

'All right.'

She wondered if he remembered what he had promised about her own private concert, but didn't think it was the time to ask. He started the engine, and gave her a bleak nod of farewell, and drove off towards the main road. She walked back across the graveyard, still clutching her bunch of roses, and went back into the church, wondering what miracles had happened to him, to make him so sure they existed. Perhaps to be playing in the Festival Hall at Old-bridge when he was so young. Being married to Ruth, perhaps. Perhaps she would find out one day.

She did the flowers, putting the new roses on the altar. In spite of the fact they were not gold or silver or jewelled plate, they glowed in the afternoon sunlight with colours as godly as any precious stones, and the maggot holes didn't show at all. For saying prayers, not many had a virtual cathedral of their own to hear their desires ... Marion went down on her knees in front of the altar. Usually she used a pew, if she just felt like saying something friendly, or wanting something not very important, but for the church itself the altar steps seemed right. It was just a matter, really, of formalizing what God knew already she wanted so badly, and adding about the rich American, and a bit for Pat himself.

She prayed as well as she knew how. Not exactly the words —it was the intensity of the feelings one put into it; if the praying was really good, one felt quite tired afterwards, in Marion's rather limited experience. She had just about finished, and was winding up with a few thank-yous—not purely sycophantic, but true thank-yous; including one for introducing her to Pat and Ruth (especially Pat)—when the latch on the door dropped with a clatter and she heard some-one come in. She scrambled up, not wanting to be caught in the act, and scurried down the nave, hoping to pass the visitor and escape without saying anything. The visitor was looking up at the roof and muttering to himself, but some-thing in his muttering struck Marion as quite extraordinary.

'God dammit, I've never seen anything so bee-ootiful. . . .'

The fact that he was talking to himself was quite irrele-vant; it was the broad nasal intonation that so stunned Marion, the unmistakably American accent, delivered on the heels of her final amen at the altar steps. God might move in a mysterious way, but that he could move so *fast* was almost unbelievable. She stopped in her tracks and stared.

'Hi, kid,' the man said. 'You live around here?'

He was small and wiry, fiftyish, Marion thought, with a strong, impressive nose and very lively, quick eyes. He had crinkly black hair going grey, a kind, mobile mouth. He wore a short white raincoat, immaculately pressed, a light tobacco-brown suit, and he had a jaunty hat of pale suede with a tiny gold feather. Round his neck hung an extremely impressive-looking camera. He looked, in short, like a very rich American.

Marion, wasting no time, said, 'Yes, it's very beautiful but it's in a bad state of repair. It might have to be closed if

49

we can't get enough money to fix it.'

'Is that so?' His eyes, removing themselves momentarily from the roof, fixed on her with interest. They then went back to the roof, and visibly filled with undeniable grief.

'That would be a tragedy! I've never seen anything so lovely as those carved angels.'

He stood and gazed slowly round the whole church, the quick eyes darting over every crack and damp-stain. He started to walk slowly down the aisle, gazing up at the roof. Marion walked by his side. Pair by pair the aloof angels spread their wings over their footsteps. The American studied them intently, pair by pair. He fetched out gold-rimmed spectacles from his pocket and fixed them over the great arch of his nose. He had very delicate nostrils, flared like shells.

'What do you know about this church?' he asked her. 'About these angels?'

Marion told him everything she knew. They mounted the altar steps together and turned as if to bless a congregation, standing together. The man listened very intently, not at all impatient, deeply—flatteringly—interested. Marion talked with the same ardour as she had so recently used in her prayers, feeling that this man was a challenge to her powers of persuasion, a part of God's plan for St. Michael's. She was convinced that he had been sent, that he was going to get out his cheque-book and write her a cheque for seven hundred and fifty thousand pounds as soon as her eloquence had made itself felt.

'Well, well, well,' he said. 'You sure know your facts, honey. You're some scholar, I'll say that for you. You the priest's daughter or some'n?'

'No.'

'You sure can talk. How come you know all that?'

'I look after it,' she said.

'You do?' The intent gaze turned back to her, amused,

impressed. '*You?*'

'Yes.'

'Don't they have a Committee of Friends? No ladies running coffee-parties to raise funds? Nobody from some institution or some'n to look after it?'

'No.'

'You British—you treat history like it's some'n that's just lying around, take it or leave it ... you got those God-darned angels up there and nobody's interested? I just don't believe that, honey.'

'No, well, they're *interested*, but they say it's going to cost too much to repair the church and it will probably have to be closed, and the tower demolished.'

'Gee, that's terrible. A place like this. This place is magnificent. I sure wouldn't mind taking this home with me.'

Marion's heart lurched with horror, remembering that Americans were inclined to do that sort of thing: she had heard of it, removing old buildings stone by stone, all numbered and labelled, for re-erection in Texas or Kansas or somewhere equally unlikely. She saw St. Michael's standing in the American's backyard, lined up with the swimming-pool and the tennis-court, shining and incongruous in Californian sunshine. God was letting things go astray.

'You can't take it home!'

'No, baby, but I sure wouldn't like it to fall down because you British don't know how to look after your history.'

'We do know. We just haven't got enough money.'

'How much money d'you say?'

'Seven hundred and fifty thousand pounds.'

'That sure is a lot of cash. You can say that again.'

He looked thoughtful. Marion waited for him to produce his cheque-book, but nothing happened. He glanced at his watch.

Marion said, desperately, 'If you think it's so beautiful,

couldn't you—wouldn't you like to—' Desperate as she was, she couldn't actually say it. She shut her eyes and prayed. Standing on the altar steps, she prayed so hard that the sweat came out in little beads all across her forehead.

When she opened her eyes, the American was looking at her in a very curious way.

'Are you okay, honey?'

'Yes.'

'What you want for this church, honey, is a bit of publicity. I might be able to raise you a bit of publicity. I'll have a word with my agent.'

Marion wasn't sure if her prayer was working or not. She couldn't exactly see how, but it sounded right somehow.

'I'm on holiday right now. Six months rest, they said. But my agent's over here with me—he don't believe in resting much. I'll have a word with him and see what he says. I'd like to do a little thing like that. I don't want six months rest, like my agent. We're used to working.'

Marion was lost.

'A few little concerts perhaps, with a whole lot of publicity.'

'*Concerts?*' Marion grasped the familiar straw. Of course, the festival ... Oldbridge was swarming with musicians this week, Americans, Europeans, Japanese, Pennington....

'We had one—a concert, to make money. But it only makes a little bit—you need dozens, hundreds—'

'No, honey, not the way we do it. You do a few concerts. You get your publicity right. You make your appeal. The concert just starts things rolling. My agent knows the job backwards. We'd raise you the money, if we put our minds to it.'

'Do you play the piano?'

'No, honey. I'm a fiddler.' He produced a card from his wallet, with a name and address on it. It was a foreign-looking name: Ephraim Voigt.

'You'd want an orchestra?' Marion was remembering about the expenses, eating up all the lovely money.

'No, baby. Just an accompanist.'

'A pianist? I know a pianist.'

He laughed. 'Whadyer know? It's in the bag.' He clapped her on the shoulder. 'I must be getting along. I'll miss the concert.'

'That's him! The pianist—I know him! You're going to the concert, now? At the Festival Hall?'

'That's right.'

'Well, he's the pianist I know. He likes this church too. He comes here. He was here earlier. He would accompany you.'

'You don't say! I'll go and see how he sounds!'

Marion couldn't tell whether the man was just having her on, or whether he meant it. She walked back down the aisle with him as she had walked with Patrick earlier, and he kept up his gee-whizzing about the angels, his big nose angled up to the roof. He took some photographs, exploding magnesium flashes into the ether enough to startle the whole dozen into flight, then some in the churchyard; then he clapped her on the shoulder again and drove away in a car about four times the length of Pat's with room for about ten people inside.

Marion watched him go, and sat on a tombstone, her legs feeling suddenly very weak. The place was deserted, silent, basking in the afternoon sun. She couldn't believe any of it had happened at all. She thought she must have fallen asleep over her prayers, trying so hard, and dreamed it all. But the visiting card was in her hand. Her hand was trembling. She felt exhausted, shattered.

She felt so ill she started to cry. She realized she was getting into one of her states, and forced herself to her feet, and stumbled back to the cottage and down the garden.

53

'Daddy! Daddy!'

'What's the matter?'

Recognizing the need he climbed down off his boat and she flung herself on him, burying her face in his tattered shirt. He put his arms round her and waited. His familiar smell, of marine ply and epoxy resin, soothed her. He stroked her hair and said, 'Let's sit on the bank for a bit, then we'll go and make a cup of tea. You can tell me what's set you off.'

They sat on a corner of the cockpit cover, and looked out over the smooth banks of mud and the brown tide pushing its way up its channel in the middle; like gravy, Marion always thought, a scum on its edges, questing and worrying its way inland. The golden samphire was wiry under their feet, fringing the top lip of the bank.

'I went in the church and Pat was there.' She told him exactly what had happened. She showed him the visiting card.

'Ephraim Voigt,' Geoff read. 'Well, even I have heard of him.'

'What do you mean?'

'He's a violinist.'

'That's what he said.'

'Just about the most famous violinist in the world.'

Marion could see that even Geoff was shaken this time. He sat staring at the card, and frowned out over the river.

'Even if Pat does believe in miracles,' he said, 'I reckon he'll be a bit surprised by this one.'

'Do you think it's a miracle?'

'It's a coincidence. Just how far coincidences have to go to become miracles—your guess is as good as mine.'

'He might just have—well, he might forget. We might never hear from him again. Perhaps I only thought he said all that.'

'Quite possibly. But he was there.'

54

'Yes.'

'Although half the famous musicians in the world are at Oldbridge this week . . . well, one or two.' Geoff was chewing a grass, still frowning.

'We'd better forget it,' he said. 'Unless he follows it up. I wouldn't count on that.'

'No.'

'It is extraordinary, there's no doubt.'

They went up the garden, and Geoff put the kettle on. When the tea was made and they were sitting on the doorstep in the sun to drink it, Geoff said, 'It might be best not to tell anyone what happened. Not about your praying, I mean. All right about meeting the man in the church, but not about him coming in answer to a prayer.'

'Nobody would believe it.'

'No.'

Marion knew that he was thinking that everyone would mark it against her, another bit of evidence of how peculiar she was.

'Pat knows. It was his idea.'

'Oh, yes. *We* know—' It was odd, Marion thought, how Pat and Ruth were already accepted into this especially intimate relationship, not particularly because of this incident, but because, somehow, they fitted. Like old shoes. They had arrived, and they seemed to be on the same wavelength as her and Geoff which, mostly, was a slightly different one from other peoples'.

'We know,' he repeated. 'But people like Alfred, Mrs. Rowley and them—don't say anything. Pat's all right. You can tell him.'

'I prayed for him to do well in his concert too, so perhaps that worked as well. He looked a bit—a bit nervous. He told me to.'

'Yes, I daresay. I wouldn't like to do what he does. I

hope it worked for him.'

'Yes. I like him. Ever so. And her.'

'Mmm.'

'You know—' She paused, glanced sideways at Geoff. 'She reminds me—' She stopped. 'You said she did too.'

Geoff was drinking his tea. He put the empty mug down. 'Yes. Not the looks, exactly. But the way she—' He wasn't sure, and hesitated.

'The way she is,' Marion said.

'I suppose.'

He smiled suddenly and said, 'Did you say any prayers for me while you were about it?'

'No. I'm sorry.'

'If my prayers were to come true, it wouldn't solve anything.' Geoff spoke obscurely, quietly. Sometimes he said things Marion didn't understand, but she got him puzzled too at times; it was mutual. But nothing to worry about. She looked at him sideways, the familiar, rather bony profile, a few freckles, sawdust, untidy blond hair. He didn't look like a father, somehow. Not like the sort that came to school to meetings. He never came to the meetings. 'They'll tell me, if I need to know anything,' he always said hopefully.

'You could pray for my beam-shelf, next time,' he said. 'God might know where that extra two inches on the starboard side came from. I'm sure I don't.'

She helped him for the rest of the afternoon, and the shock of what had happened receded. They could easily have dismissed it altogether, save for the card standing on the mantelpiece in the kitchen.

Quite late, when Marion was undressing for bed, the phone rang. Geoff answered it. She heard him say, 'Just a moment. I'll fetch her.'

He put his head round the stairs door and called up. 'Marion, it's your American.'

56

She came down in her vest, her heart bumping.

'Hullo?'

'You the little girl in the church this afternoon? I rang the padre and he gave me your number. Is that you, honey?'

'Yes.'

'Well, it's okay, sweetheart. I had a word with my agent. He thinks it's a cute idea. And your friend—I sat in on his concert, and he's okay too. Real nice playing for such a kid. Now I'll leave it to you to tell him what's cooking, eh? You tell him to contact my agent. He might not want to do it —well, I can send home for my usual guy if not. We can discuss it any time he likes. Can I leave that to you? To get him to contact my agent?'

'Yes.'

'As soon as you like. I don't know how he's fixed. He'll have to let us know. I'm staying at the George. You can get me there, leave a message any time. You'll do that, honey?'

'Yes.'

'Fine. See you.'

He rang off. Marion stood in her vest, holding the receiver, rooted to the ground. Geoff took it off her, gently, and put it back on its rest.

'It's come true, your miracle? What did he say?'

'He said yes. He'd do it. The concerts . . . he wants Pat to accompany him. He told me to tell him.'

She looked at her father, white-faced.

'I feel queer.'

'You're not the only one,' Geoff murmured. He put his arm round her, and could feel his own hand not entirely steady. He didn't want to say anything to alarm her, but. . . .

'Stone the crows, Marion, you must have prayed damned hard.'

'I did. It made me come out in a sweat.'

'You want to be careful.' He tried to make it sound like

57

a joke. But miracles couldn't be turned into jokes.

'It is a miracle, isn't it?' Marion wanted to be sure.

'If it isn't, it's the closest thing to a miracle I've come across.'

He guided her across to the kitchen table and pressed her into a chair. Then he sat down opposite her.

'He was going to come and visit that church anyway, whether you'd prayed or not. You were in there, and he was coming. The fact that you prayed, and then he came—that was a coincidence. That's my story, anyway. Don't get worried about it, Marion.'

'No, I'm not worried.'

After the first shock had worn off it was true. She smiled blissfully.

'If it all happens, like he says, the church will be all right!'

'They know a thing or two about fund-raising, those Americans. It could well happen.'

'I must go and see Pat.' She started to get off the chair but her father pressed her back.

'Not now! Why've you got to see him?'

'He left it to me, to tell him. He said he listened to his concert, and he was good, and I must tell him to contact his agent, and see if he wants to do it. Otherwise he'll send home for his usual guy.'

'I wonder what Pat'll think of that?'

'*He* told me to pray for a rich American. It's all his fault really.'

Geoff grinned. 'I'd like to see his face!'

'Can we go in the morning, first thing? It's terribly important.'

'Yes, you'd better take the morning off school. I can't come. I've got to go and see a bloke in Cambridge at ten. I'll drop you at the bus-stop. They're in that cottage at the far end of the beach, the one old Mr. Nipsell owns.'

'I know.'

They both sat back in their chairs, awed by the day's events. It was no good trying to pretend that what had happened was ordinary run-of-the-mill Sunday goings-on. Whichever way you looked at it, miracle or coincidence, the effect was likely to be stupendous. They sat for some time in complete silence.

Then, to be on the safe side, Geoff gave Marion two aspirins with a glass of water, and chivvied her off to bed.

Chapter Four

Marion was very nervous of going to see Pat in the morning. She had no idea what her reception would be, even whether he would believe her. But her instructions had been quite clear. The message must be delivered.

Geoff said, 'He'll be in a good mood if he's read the papers. Look at this.' He pointed out a passage amongst the reviews in the morning newspaper from which Marion gathered, for it was very technical, that his playing of the second Brahms piano concerto had been well received.

'Lyrical, joyous playing. . . .' He had seemed to her neither lyrical nor joyous when she had met him. Perhaps working up to being lyrical and joyous on the keyboard was very hard work. But possibly her prayers for him had been as successful as the prayer for the rich American.

'It's all his fault, after all, what's happened. It's him who said pray for a rich American.'

Geoff laughed. 'Off you go then. He can hardly be displeased, if the best violinist in the world wants him as an accompanist.'

'Who said he's the best violinist in the world?'

'I did. He must be, if I've heard of him.'

Marion decided not to go too early, in case Pat was having a long lie in bed after his ordeal. She caught the bus at half-past nine and walked slowly when she got to Oldbridge, looking in all the shop-windows. It was all health-food shops and crusty bread, and sailing clothes and funny coloured wool. The town was full of retired admirals and old, fit ladies with thick white hair and strong dogs on leads. Behind the shops the sea crashed on the steep, shingly beach. Oldbridge so far had not been taken by the sea like its one-time neighbour a few miles farther on, but the sea was very close. Hungry, Marion thought. Eating at the stones. It wasn't a very good bathing beach, too steep and uncomfortable. But nice and scrunchy to walk on, and amiable dogs chased the seagulls and nosed out dead herrings from round the fishermen's huts.

Pat's house, a cottage called Fair Winds, was out beyond the end of the sea-walk, where the sand dunes took over and the shingle gave way to a sort of grit, half-way to sand. It was very exposed, and bleak in bad weather, but a very desirable spot in the sunshine. It was almost sunshine now, a pearly, pale day with the sea and the sky merging. Marion walked where the sea licked at her sandals; beyond the town the beach was less steep and the sea farther away. She was spinning out the walk, nervous, trying to make sense of yesterday. Today nothing seemed less likely than a miracle. Today was excessively ordinary; you could look round the whole horizon, land and sea, and spot nothing even faintly unusual. There seemed to be several people sitting in deck-chairs on the beach outside Fair Winds, more than just Pat and Ruth: but even that could hardly be considered unusual, considering it was Festival week and musicians, presumably, liked to get together and talk. However, it was a little off-putting. Marion walked more and more slowly.

There were four people, in fact, three men and Ruth. None of the men were Pat. Marion had come to a complete halt, taking in the scene, when Ruth saw her and got up with a cheerful wave.

'Marion! Are you looking for us?'

She came towards her, brown legs under a red towelling coat. Marion did not move. Ruth was laughing.

'Come on. They don't bite.'

Marion had to advance, there being no alternative, and

was introduced to the three men.

'This is Mr. Crocker, who used to teach Pat when he was at school.'

Marion bent down to shake hands, Mr. Crocker being rather old and fragile-looking, like a gnome, with a lot of untidy white hair and a wrinkled smile.

'Pleased to meet you, my dear.'

'And this is Professor Hampton, who used to teach Pat when he had left school.'

Professor Hampton, not quite so elderly, was a bit frightening, smooth and elegant, his smile charming but without warmth. He did not get up, but offered up a white, bony hand. Marion could feel herself blushing, wishing she hadn't got her jeans all wet.

'And this is Mick, Pat's agent.'

Mick had been sitting on the sand but got up and took her hand as if he had been waiting for her, making her feel like a queen. He was young and striking, with hair like a lion's mane, and very beautiful but untidy clothes.

'You're the girl with a whole church to herself?' he said. His voice was foreign, but the accent wasn't recognizable to Marion. She hadn't imagined that agents looked anything like this; she had imagined them hard-faced and cigar-smoking, sitting at a desk making tough deals on the telephone. She was a bit thrown about his knowing about the church, then remembered that it was he who had arranged

the concert; Pat had said so, in despair, when he had discovered he was playing for charity. This was the man who would have to go and see Mr. Voigt.

But she wasn't going to tell anyone else first.

'I've come to see Pat,' she said.

'Oh. He's out there somewhere.' Mick waved an arm out to sea, and everyone turned round to look.

'He's been gone a long time,' the Professor said. 'You aren't very diligent in keeping an eye on your valuable property.'

'He's always a long time,' Ruth said.

'Swimming—we don't worry about him swimming, even when it's rough,' Mick said. 'That fast car now—that's another matter.'

Ruth grinned. 'Your car is just as fast, and you don't drive it as well.'

'Ah, but I'm expendable,' Mick said.

There was a swimmer, Marion could see now, quite far out. So far out that her heart sank slightly, wondering how ever she could keep her end up with these smart people until Pat came. But Ruth saved her by saying, 'Come with me, Marion, and we'll make coffee and bring it out on the beach. Pat will be back by then.'

They scrambled back over the dunes towards the cottage, collecting Lud on the way, who was covered in sand, looking furry and gold like a teddy-bear.

'There's nothing wrong, is there?' Ruth asked. 'You look worried.'

'No. I don't think so.'

This reply baffled Ruth, but she didn't nose, measuring coffee into a large percolator. The cottage was very untidy but comfortable-looking—rather in the same way as Marion's own home—and the living-room was largely taken up with an enormous piano, so that the bit left for living in was very small.

'It's nice here,' Marion said. At the back there was a creek, winding through spongy grass, cutting the cottage off from the coast road, keeping it private.

'Yes, I like it. Better than London. I want to stay, but it's a bit awkward for Pat, travelling. It's so far away from anywhere really. He likes driving, luckily.'

Lud sat at the table, eating a biscuit, staring at Marion with stern, impassive eyes. He looked like Pat.

'You can carry the sugar,' Ruth said to him. Very trusting, Marion thought, for such a difficult journey over dunes. 'Don't get sand in it. The Professor won't like it. They came for the concert yesterday,' she added to Marion. 'They like taking the credit, when he's good, you see. Quite understandable really. Will you carry the percolator? I'll take the tray.'

Marion picked it up.

'He *was* good—the paper said so. Daddy showed me.'

'Yes.'

'I've got a message for him. I had to come.'

'Take Marion's hand, Lud,' Ruth said.

His hand was soft and gritty and trusting. Marion liked it, matching her pace to his, watching the sugar tightly clutched. They mounted the dunes, and saw Pat coming up the beach.

'Daddy!' Lud shouted, pulling suddenly. Marion rescued the sugar just in time. It was demerara, and the sand didn't show. Lud raced down the beach and Pat caught him and lifted him on to his shoulders. It was odd, seeing him in his father role, not screwed-up and serious any more, but laughing. 'It's Marion!' he said.

Marion felt herself going scarlet again, because he seemed genuinely pleased to see her, and she was so frightened about her message. He only had to say no, if he didn't want to; she didn't know why she was frightened. Only because of the whole thing, the miracle ... you would be stupid, really, not to be nervous of miracles.

'What are you doing here?'

'I've got a message for you. I had to come.'

'Good. Who from?' He came up and sat down next to Mick, tumbling Lud into his lap. He looked up at her. 'God?'

Ruth threw a towel at him. 'Sit down, Marion. I'm sorry there are no more chairs. Put the percolator on the tray.'

Marion did as she was told, and muttered to Pat, 'It's from a man called Ephraim Voigt.'

Pat put Lud down rather suddenly and looked at her closely.

'Are you serious?'

'Yes.'

He picked up the towel and rubbed at his face, regarding her over the top of it, only the eyes showing. They were very intent.

'Have you met him?'

'He came into the church, yesterday.'

Marion knew that Pat realized what she was saying, what she hadn't said, in fact, although the others had overheard the American's name and obviously, like her father, had no trouble in recognizing it.

'After I left you?'

'Yes.'

'After you had prayed?' He said it in a whisper.

'Yes,' she whispered back.

'Jesus,' he said into the towel. His eyes disappeared as he started to rub his hair.

'Voigt's here for the Festival,' the Professor said. 'I saw him in Oldbridge yesterday.'

'He was at the concert,' Mick said. He leaned across to look at Marion and said, 'You say he had a message for Pat?'

'He wants him to contact him—or you, that is. His agent. To contact his agent.'

'Why?'

'He wants Pat to play with him.'

She was telling it all wrong. She should have said it to Pat privately, how it had come about. They were all staring at her in astonishment, poised over the coffee-cups.

'Why?' Mick asked. 'What for? Why Pat?'

Pat said, coming out of the towel, 'It's for the church, isn't it? You told him. He came in and you told him?'

'Yes.'

The others didn't understand, but she could see that Pat knew exactly what had happened without being told. It was part of the old thing, that she felt she knew Pat very well indeed, that she had always known him, and now it was reciprocal. She didn't have to explain all the details to him, because he already knew.

Mick was asking, 'Why did he want Pat?'

'Because Marion told him,' Pat said.

'He was on his way to the concert anyway,' Marion said, not wanting to be responsible for everything. 'I only told him that you liked the church too, and had already played a concert to raise money.'

'And he said, "I'll go and listen and see if he's any good, and if he is he can accompany me."'

'Instead of his usual guy.'

'Instead of his usual guy,' Pat repeated.

'And last night, late, he rang up and said—' She paused.

'Go on. What did he say?'

'He said—' She looked up from the sand, saw they were all hanging on her words, and felt the blushes flooding her yet again. '"Real nice playing for—"'

'For what?'

'"For such a kid."'

67

Pat's face was expressionless, but all the others laughed. She could see that they were amazed, and excited. The miracle was real, rubbed off on these know-alls too.

'The publicity would be fantastic,' Mick said.

'Exactly how would it help the church?' Ruth asked. 'One or two concerts, even with him, don't make seven hundred and fifty thousand pounds.'

'He said, "You do a few concerts. You get your publicity right. You make your appeal. The concerts just start things rolling." He said his agent knows the job backwards.'

'He's got the name and the influence to do it,' Mick said. 'When he plays over here, there's never an empty seat. Even with charity concert prices, it will be the same. And then, if he makes the appeal, and his publicity machine gets to work, and the church people do some of the spadework, I reckon you'd raise your money.'

'You'd better start rubbing up your Kreutzer sonata, Pat, and your César Franck,' the Professor said drily. 'I seem to remember your doing the Spring quite adequately with Clarissa in the old days. But Mr. Voigt, I imagine, will be a good deal more demanding than Miss Cargill-Smith.'

'A wonderful opportunity, working with a man of that calibre,' Mr. Crocker said, beaming. 'Extraordinary!'

'You were going to take a few weeks off after this Festival,' Ruth said to Pat flatly.

Pat stood up, the towel round his neck. 'I'm going to get dressed,' he said.

He looked down at Marion. 'Come with me. I want to talk to you.'

Marion followed him over the dunes, chastened. 'Are you cross?'

'No.'

'You haven't got to. He can't make you.'

'Mick will. I have got to.'

68

'I'm sorry. Truly. I didn't mean—'

'No, idiot. There's nothing to be sorry for. It's the other business—your praying, and him coming. Was it just like that? You prayed—'

'Yes. I prayed at the altar the minute you'd gone, and when I turned round, there he was. I couldn't believe it.'

'And you told him—?'

'Yes. I told him everything. He asked me first, he asked me about the angels, so of course I told him. I had to tell him. That's what he was there for.'

'You believe that? I told you miracles happen.'

'Yes.'

'What did Geoff say?'

'He said it was a coincidence. But getting on for a miracle.'

'I'll say! Did you pray for me too?'

'Yes.'

'You could go into business, Marion. That worked as well. Everything went right.'

'You're not cross then?'

'No.'

'You don't mind playing with Mr. Voigt?'

'You don't exactly mind, being invited to play with a person like that. That's not the feeling at all.'

'What is it then?'

'The feeling? At the moment, doubt, horror, panic, amazement ... incredulity. Gloom. The work involved—'

'That's minding, I would have said.'

'Oh, no. That's normal. Later on, I shall feel better about it. If it looks like coming true—well then, I might start feeling a bit excited.'

Marion was infinitely relieved. 'I felt so awful, coming here, to tell you.'

'You really are a nut,' he said.

They went into the kitchen, and he perched on the table

and ate a biscuit out of a packet Ruth had left open. He was brown and hefty in his nakedness, and wore a gold medallion round his neck on a chain. Having got her ordeal over, Marion realized she was once more blissfully happy.

'You are pleased? Really, underneath?'

'You might say, not displeased. Flattered. Frightened.'

'He seemed very nice to me.'

'No doubt. I only know him by reputation.'

'What's his reputation?'

'Fierce. Great. God's not doing this thing by halves, sending Mr. Voigt in answer to your prayers.' He took another biscuit. 'It's a very queer thing. Does anybody else know?'

'Daddy said not to say anything. He said to you, it didn't matter, but not anybody else.'

'No. You'll get burnt for a witch.'

'Not for having prayers answered!'

'No. Sorry. Made into a saint. I've got it the wrong way round. Saint Marion. Sounds funny. I'll go and get dressed.'

He slipped off the table and went upstairs and the ceiling creaked as he moved about the bedroom. Marion went into the living-room, where the watery, greenish sun washed over the ebony Steinway. Dog-eared sheets of music stood in piles, mixed up with Lud's toy cars and bricks, and some knitting and a bowl of oranges. It was a very nice room, Marion thought, as if everyone did their own thing in amicable companionship. At home, with only her and Geoff, there weren't enough of them to get this feeling.

Pat came down, in jeans and a blue T-shirt, his hair slicked smooth with a comb. His hands, sea-washed, were large and articulate, spread over the keys.

'I'm sorry but I've got to work now.'

'It's all right—I can tell Mr. Voigt it's all right?'

'Yes. Mick will see to it. Go and arrange it with Mick.'

He seemed to have lost interest, frowning at the music on the rest in front of him. But as she hesitated, he looked up and said, 'If this thing happens, and I meet him, and it's all right, you can be in on it too. You can come over, and Geoff too, if he wants. We could all have supper, when this Festival week is over.'

'And my concert—?' Her voice was almost a whisper.

'Yes.' He smiled. 'I promise.'

She went back over the dunes to the others, who were all talking with considerable animation about Ephraim Voigt's invitation and its likely consequences. The talk was technical and involved. The only opinion Marion fully understood was Ruth's, who was saying fiercely to Mick, 'Three weeks clear, without any engagements—just coming up . . . and now this! He needs a break! *I* need him—I need him for three weeks. I did so want it!'

'It's great, Ruthie—you know it is. You don't pass over opportunities in this business.'

'He isn't an accompanist, anyway—'

'He's a musician, Ruth. He's a great pianist, and that's what Voigt wants.'

Ruth made a face. 'I know what it will mean. Work, work, work.'

'Is that anything new?'

'Oh, after the Brahms, month in, month out, for two—three—years . . . no—what's a potty sonata or two? I just think, sometimes, I married a Steinway, that's all.'

'It's paying off, Ruthie. You know it is. You don't get notices like he got today just sitting making daisy-chains.'

'Oh—' Ruth gathered up the cups angrily. 'It's not *every-thing*—'

'It is, just now, you know it is.' Mick's voice was gentle and quite ruthless at the same time.

Ruth tried to get the percolator on the tray and couldn't.

71

Marion bent down and took it off her. 'I'll help you.'

Ruth was close to tears. She got up and started back over the dunes. Marion hurried after her, cold with remorse. It was no good asking Ruth if she minded, for she quite clearly did. Marion couldn't think of anything adequate to say at all. They went into the kitchen. Great floods of piano-music reverberated through the whole house; Ruth kicked the door to the living-room shut, but it didn't make much difference. Ruth started to run the water into the sink, but the tears were rolling down her cheeks.

'Don't take any notice of me,' she said to Marion. 'I'll be all right in a minute. It was just—' She stopped.

'I really am sorry,' Marion whispered.

Ruth piled the cups and saucers into the bowl. Then she turned round to Marion: 'Look, you mustn't mind. I'm stupid. Once I prayed as hard as you—every night—for Pat's career to be a success.'

'How do you know I prayed?'

'Pat told me, last night. After he had played so well. He made a joke of it, said it was because you prayed for him. But I've heard him play it as well as that without prayers.'

'Did he tell you I was going to pray for a rich American?'

'Yes.'

'I wouldn't have, if I'd known—'

'No. Don't say that. It is a very great compliment, a great opportunity, just like Mick says. I should be very pleased. I am, really, but I just would have liked a week or two first, without any pressures—I was so looking forward to it. He had promised, you see—three weeks, we had kept it free. No engagements, minimal practising. So I'm disappointed. And it is terribly selfish of me—to be cross about such a marvellous thing for him, so that makes me feel even worse. I'm just a mess really. Don't take any notice.'

'I don't think you're a mess,' Marion said, anguished.

Even prayers wouldn't work this one out. 'Perhaps you can still have the three weeks—there might not be any great hurry?'

'Possibly. But with Mick making the arrangements, it's not likely.' She smiled, doubtfully. 'Anyway, it's splendid news—it really could save the church, couldn't it? We can always have our holiday once this is worked out. Please don't worry, Marion. I'm sorry I'm such a wet blanket. You don't deserve it.'

She was back to normal, reaching for the detergent.

'I'll just do these things, then I'll dress Lud and go back with you along the beach. I've got to do some shopping. We can have an ice-cream in The Copper Kettle. Would you like that?'

'Oh, yes, I would.'

'And Mick will run you home when you want. It's the least he can do, after all you've done for us.'

And Marion waited, doing the drying up. She saw that Pat, engaged with his piano, wasn't any sort of a companion at all. Even when he was at home. And the rest of the time he was travelling to engagements. And Ruth was, strangely, as lonely as Geoff at times. She remembered the description of Swithin: 'He lived for his werke and took no wyf,' and how Ruth had remarked upon it, when they had talked in the churchyard. It fitted in a very curious way. All this thing, saving the church and the angels, was for Swithin really. Waiting for Ruth, Marion found herself watching Pat at the piano, through the glass panes of the dividing door. He was Swithin again, in her mind, the way he looked; he was as remote, unknowable; absorbed, dedicated ... it gave her an uneasy, rather frightened, cold feeling, to be so deeply involved in relationships outside her understanding. She hadn't *meant*, praying, to make Ruth cry, to summon the greatest violinist in the world ... was it all getting a little out of hand, perhaps? It was slightly ominous, standing there waiting, to feel that she had set in train events that might, in the end, involve far more than the welfare of the twelve carved angels.

Chapter Five

Marion, having reported fairly fully to Geoff the result of her visit to Fair Winds, was relieved to hear no more until the following week. Alfred, it appeared, had had a mysterious message from someone whom he said sounded like an American, asking if he had any objections to his church getting a bit of publicity, as some well-wishers wanted to get up an appeal. He had, rather nervously, said no. Two days after this the local paper appeared with excited headlines: 'American boost for decaying St. Michael's:Ephraim Voigt to play.' The following day even the most discreet of the national dailies ran the story. Some rhapsodized about St. Michael's and 'the forlorn grandeur of the village cathedral dominating the serpentine estuary, clustered around with thatched, rose-covered cottages straight out of Patience Strong.'

'Who's Patience Strong?' Marion asked belligerently.

'A lady who wrote poems.'

They pored over the printed story, impressed by the evidence that the plan was actually taking shape:

Ephraim Voigt, leading American violinist, resting in England for six months on doctor's advice, has decided to espouse the cause of St. Michael's, a semi-derelict fifteenth-century church in East Anglia. Seven hundred and fifty thousand pounds is required to restore the church to make it safe. Said Mr. Voigt last night: 'I cannot bear to think of this irreplaceable roof being allowed to fall in through neglect and lack of funds. What better way to pay my respects to this lovely country of yours than to lead an appeal to save this beautiful church?'

Voigt is arranging to play charity concerts for St. Michael's in London, Cambridge and Norwich. He has invited the young virtuoso pianist Patrick Pennington to accompany him in a programme of Beethoven sonatas. Mr. Pennington said in London last night, 'I am delighted and honoured by the invitation.'

75

'He never!' Marion said. 'I asked him what he thought and he said the panics—horror, he said. Gloom. Amazement.'

'Oh, well, that's not what you say to a newspaper, nit-wit.'

'And Ruth cried.'

'That wouldn't make a good story at all.' Geoff paused and grinned. 'The best story is yours—conjuring that American out of thin air with your prayers. Lucky the papers don't know the real truth of it! You'd have reporters queuing all down the lane.'

Shortly after they had read the story in the paper, Ruth rang up:

'There's a dinner at the George, and we've all got to go —it's another publicity do. You're both to come. Ephraim's most emphatic.'

'Oh, my Gawd,' Geoff said. 'Must we?'

'Well, it's for the church. That's what I keep telling Pat. You must come, you and Marion. More than anybody.'

'Very well. We are delighted and honoured by the

invitation.'

Ruth giggled. 'Mick told him what to say. It's terribly useful to have someone to tell you what to say. Tonight then—eight o'clock.'

'We'll be there.'

Geoff put down the receiver and explained gloomily to Marion what was expected of them.

'What are you going to wear?' he said, worried. 'It'll all be terribly smart.'

'Not that awful shiny dress.'

'You look a sight in it. Perhaps Carol—Miss Foster—she found you something for the school theatre trip. We really must go shopping one day, Marion.'

'Ugh.'

'Ask Miss Foster.'

'All right.'

Miss Foster was her teacher at school. She was sympathetic to Marion's problems, and used to rather odd appeals from Geoff. Marion had heard it said by several people that Geoff and Miss Foster made a good pair; people said that Miss Foster liked Geoff, and 'he could do a lot worse than remarry with a nice girl like her.' But Marion knew that it had never crossed Geoff's mind.

Asking her about something to wear, Marion looked at her closely, working out if she'd like to have her round the house all day, married to Geoff. Carol Foster was slightly plump, brisk and cheerful and very easy to get on with, but Marion thought, on the whole, no. At least, yes for a lot of things, like getting the tea and supplying the right sort of clothes, but not for sitting on the kitchen steps drinking cups of tea and not saying anything much. Funnily enough, Marion could see Ruth doing that very well. Even supplying the right clothes, rather peculiar ones like her own, but undeniably right.

'Well, look, Marion, I'll ask Mrs. Rowley at lunch-time.
Melissa's your size. I'm sure she'll find something. Don't
worry about it. I'll bring something after lunch
and you can try it on. I can take up a hem if necessary.
Why have they asked you then? Because you look after the
church?'

'Yes. And I know Mrs. Pennington. She asked me.'

She felt like saying, 'God asked me, because I arranged
it all,' but didn't.

Mrs. Rowley sent a perfectly suitable, frightfully boring
dress with a cardigan to match and a pair of slimy sandals
with silver buckles.

'You look super,' Carol said.

Marion didn't agree, but pretended to. Geoff said she
looked like the head girl. Marion said he looked like the
bank manager. He wore a dark grey suit that he had worn
at Liz's funeral and a pale blue tie he borrowed from Horry.
'We really must do something about our wardrobes some-
time, Marion,' he said, but she knew he never would. They
drove to Oldbridge and arrived at the George at two minutes
to eight. Pat and Ruth were just getting out of their fast
car in the car park and Pat said to Geoff, 'I must have a
pint before I meet the Bishop and his gang. We've time for
a quick one in the Red Lion. What do you say?'

Geoff was far more at home in the Red Lion than the
George and they all went in gratefully, to find courage for
the evening before them.

'I don't mind playing a sonata or two for your rotten
church,' Pat told Marion. 'But I hate all this guff that goes
with it. What's wrong with you tonight? You look like a
banana.'

'It's this dress.'

'Oh—well—I like bananas.'

He was wearing a very severe and perfect suit, and Ruth

had a long dark dress printed all over with red poppies. Marion thought she looked fantastic.

'I wish I had a dress like that!'

'Do you? I'll make you one, if you like.'

'Really?'

'You can choose the material, and I'll make it, yes. If Geoff approves.'

Geoff obviously approved, Marion thought, pleased. He was looking at Ruth in a very odd way. As if she was his boat, with admiration and love. No, not love, Marion decided, for Ruth belonged to Pat. Like then. He liked her. We all like her.

She was saying, 'We're sorry about tonight, but it was out of our control. If you like, tomorrow, you can come to supper at home, properly—I mean, just friendly. Ephraim will have gone by then—won't he, Pat?'

'I sincerely hope so.'

'Because, apart from Ephraim and practising the sonatas, we've still got three weeks more or less off.'

'Speak for yourself,' Pat said. 'If that's *off*. . . .'

'No, well. You'll be at home, I mean.'

'Yes.'

'Tomorrow then, for supper. If you come early we can go for a walk first, along the beach. Work up an appetite.'

'Thank you. Yes, we'll come.'

Dinner at the George was nothing like so casual, as they could sense the moment they entered the hall. The bar was crowded with very smart people—'The St. Michael's appeal party?' the proprietor inquired, shepherding them to join the throng. Through double doors into the dining-room Marion could see a banqueting table laid, with a formidable array of glasses and cutlery to each place, and silver candelabra and flower arrangements and the head waiter checking. Whose money was this, she wondered? Ephraim's? Or was it

79

to be won back from the appeal?

While she was still wondering, she found herself being embraced by Ephraim himself, and much hand-shaking going on all round her—with the Bishop, the Bishop's wife, the Dean of Somewhere and his wife, Canon Somebody-or-other, Lady This and Lord That. Pat and Ruth and Geoff were all involved too, Geoff looking very much as if he wished he were working on his boat and Pat looking as if he were used to it but wishing he wasn't. Nobody, obviously, could work out where she and Geoff came into it, for Ephraim's explanation was vague; she wondered if he remembered himself, now. He wore an almost white suit, a black shirt and a silver tie, and had two very astute-looking Americans at his side, introduced as Walt and Jim—fund-raisers. Ephraim was not a bit grand in company, for all his fame, but very friendly and informal, saying, 'Yessir, I hope that's the Goddarned truth....' (what a thing to say to a Bishop, Marion was thinking!) and Marion somehow couldn't see him looking beautiful over the violin strings as Pat did over the keyboard: he had a monkey quality, she thought, long arms and long, violent fingers which he waved about when he talked. Walt and Jim were watching Pat with narrowed eyes, perhaps assessing his money-making qualities. Mick, looking incredibly elegant and artistic in fawn suede and cream silk, came to Marion and took her hand in his and kissed it and said, 'My dear little agent, I am delighted to see you again. We owe all this to you!'

'Yes,' she said, glad to receive her due recognition.

'It was very acute of you to suggest Pat to Mr. Voigt. I couldn't have been quicker myself. It will be a great opportunity for him, making American connections.'

A faint warning bell rang somewhere in the back of Marion's mind, recalling what Ruth had said about Pat's American aspirations, but at that moment dinner was announced and Pat came to her side and said to Mick, 'Excuse me, but I'm taking her in to dinner.'

Marion, wishing desperately that she didn't look like a banana, blushed with pleasure.

'Do you think Ruth really will make me a dress?'

'If she said so, she will.'

'I'd like one like hers.'

'I'm sure she can manage that.'

'Do you know which knives and forks to use?'

'Yes, I've learnt. And not to eat peas with your knife.'

They were placed impressively near the top of the table, only two from Mr. Voigt, and Geoff made sure he was next to Ruth, although Marion thought his place was meant for Mick. Mick shrewdly got himself opposite hard-eyed Walt and Jim, but had to be charming to church ladies on either hand—no problem for him; Marion thought, if you didn't know, you'd take him for the pianist and Pat for the agent. Pat and Ephraim were certainly very opposite in character; did that mean they might have difficulty playing duets?

She asked Pat.

'Quite likely,' he said gloomily. 'And as he's three times older than me and done it all ten times to my once, I shall probably have to do as I'm told.'

'But it's a great opportunity. Mick said so.'

'Yes. Mick doesn't have to do it.'

Marion, her guilt complex returning in a rush, said, 'But you don't mind? Not really? You said—'

Pat smiled and said, 'Ephraim is a great musician. My only worry is that I won't be good enough. And that I'm used to.'

'Oh, but you will.'

The dinner proceeded and Marion, eating hugely and sampling her various wine-glasses, rather lost track. She could see that her father was enjoying himself with Ruth —and the food—and that everyone, including the Bishop, was exceedingly jovial and optimistic. Only Pat at her side was quiet, abstemious, satisfied with her undemanding company. By the time they got to the dessert and the coffee and the speeches, she was feeling rather peculiar, and noticed that her father was glancing at her warily from time to time.

'If she needs fielding,' he said to Pat, 'would you—?'

'Of course.'

'I won't,' she said.

It was just the extraordinary feeling that kept coming at her in waves of talk and laughter, watching everybody, thinking of Herbert and Ted at home in the dusking canopy of the arched timber roof—that all this was because of her. She had made it, willed it. Manipulated it. Even the Bishop, making his speech, was there because she had willed it, on the altar steps. It was her miracle, although no one knew it except the four of them, her and Geoff and Pat and Ruth. Ephraim, even when he referred to her in his speech, didn't know:

'... the little lady who told me so enchantingly the sad tale of St. Michael's ...'

'... No one loves this beautiful country more than myself. It is a great honour—a delight—to do this small thing in the hope that one of the great treasures of our common past ...'

Perhaps Walt had told him what to say, Marion thought.

'... and an especial pleasure to be playing in company with one of your young and truly gifted musicians—I say this with the greatest sincerity, that I feel honoured to be partnered in this enterprise by someone young enough to dust all the cobwebs off me—someone at the start of a great career, whose generosity and—dare I say it?—bravado, in accepting the invitation of an old war-horse like me. ...'

Clapping and laughter allowed him to leave the sentence

82

hanging.

Marion saw Pat's fingers grind each other in agony under the table-cloth, and Ephraim waved his arm towards him and said, 'A few words, my boy—an accompaniment to *my* few words ... we're in this together, you know.'

More clapping and cheering, and Pat was forced to get to his feet. Marion could feel the reluctance, almost mutiny, felt her own flood of agony in sympathy, the great guilt complex again. . . .

'I think more bravado would have been required to refuse an invitation from such an old war-horse as Mr. Voigt— more a royal command than an invitation—' He paused for the gusts of sympathetic laughter and then—obviously—for inspiration, darting an appealing glance at Mick. Mick smiled somewhat anxiously and shrugged, so Pat said, 'I am afraid I'm no after-dinner speaker. I think that everybody knows that—apart from the actual piano-playing—all the work is done by my friend and business partner, Mick Zawadzki—' This also caused great amusement, and he had to pause again. 'So I think it would be best if he said a few words on my behalf, about the arrangements we have made so far with Mr. Voigt, and how we hope the appeal will work out. I will just add that I am extremely honoured to have this opportunity of working with Mr. Voigt, and only hope I will be able to justify his optimism in asking me.'

This went down very well and Pat sat down with a grunt of relief to more applause.

Mick, not reluctant at all, started to outline the arrangements and plans, tactfully deferring to Walt and Jim and making it sound as if they were the power behind the whole business.

Marion sat back, her eyes travelling down the table, taking in the involvement of all these important people, awed by what had come about. Pat had laughed and said, 'Pray for a rich American.' He had never guessed, beforehand, what was going to evolve from his instructions. He sat, like her, essentially serious amongst all the *bonhomie*, aware of the complex threads that had gone into the weaving of this enterprise—not a cause for amusement or jollity at all, but more for silent amazement. He understands, Marion thought, more of what it is all about than clever Mick with all his right words and the astute planning, and innocent Ephraim Voigt who knows nothing. We *know*, and Swithin in his grave on the cliff *knows*, and Ted and Herbert know, and God—

'Are you all right?' Geoff was leaning across the table, anxious.

Marion came back, concentrating hard.

'Yes, I think so.'

'Work at it,' Pat said. 'And then you'll be able to come to concerts. Sit in the front row.'

'Can I?'

'At the edge, near the door.'

'Please.'

He turned to her. 'You can do anything, if you want it badly enough.'

She had, after all. She had done this thing. Single-handed she had commanded this gathering and instigated the salvation of St. Michael's. She could feel herself glowing, filled with a sweet fervour, as if she would take off. Pat was looking at her very sternly.

'It's all right,' she whispered.

Pretend it's a concert, she thought, and Pat is playing. I am in the front row. And she sat tight, her feet firmly on the floor, like a rock. It was wonderful, having this feeling, and holding on. Before she had always let it run, like going downhill on a bicycle and not bothering about the consequences. But now it was different. She could work miracles; this was nothing beside what she had already done.

84

Chapter Six

The following day Marion went to Fair Winds straight from school, on the bus. Geoff said he would try and get away early, so that they could go for a walk along the beach before supper. Marion wanted to show Pat the grave, and where the old city had once stood. She got off the bus and hurried down the sea-walk, keeping to the path which ran beside the dunes, as it was quicker than the shingle. There was a large car parked outside the cottage, not Geoff's but the American ten-seater. She had forgotten all about Ephraim calling for a practice session, and slowed down abruptly. She didn't want to share Pat and Ruth with anyone else.

Lud was sitting in a large cardboard box on the grass.

'Hullo, Mari—yon.'

'Hullo, Lud.'

'That man's come.' He waved towards the car. 'An' you. Is Geoff coming?'

'Yes.'

He climbed out of the box and went to the kitchen door, battering on it with his fists.

'Mar—i—yon's come! She's come!'

Marion went in, opening the door to a smell of fried onions. Ruth was bending down to the oven, putting in a large casserole.

'Hullo! You're nice and early. I thought I'd put the dinner in to cook while we're out. That is, if Geoff can get away in time. And Ephraim goes.' The last was voiced wearily, with a wave towards the door to the living-room.

'He came at half-past one, and it's half-past four now. I didn't think he'd stay so long. I'll make a cup of tea, and

85

if I take one in to him, perhaps he'll take the hint. Are you ravenous?'

'Fairly. What are they doing?'

'Oh, they've been playing quite hard, on and off. Mostly on. It sounds lovely.' They weren't now. They were talking. 'Shall I make a sandwich to keep you going? Cheese and tomato? What about you, Lud? Want a piece of cheese?'

'Yes. Take Daddy a piece of cheese.'

'No. He's working.'

'He likes cheese.'

'Not when he's playing the piano.'

'I like cheese when I'm playing the piano.'

'Yes. Some people do. Not Daddy though.'

Lud took his cheese out to the cardboard box and got in again. Ruth made a pot of tea and opened the door to the living-room to take the tray in. Ephraim was putting his violin away in its case, a good sign. In a dark jersey and cord trousers he looked very young and agile, in spite of the grey in his hair and the face like an old brown nut.

'Hi, honey,' he said to Marion. 'Pleased to see you! You've sure set something in motion here! I feel like a new man coming to these pieces with Patrick here, and that old church to prop up—and all the nice people I've been meeting because of it. Much better than a rest—I sure do appreciate meeting you, Marion, and all you've got going for me. At my time of life, a little motivation is a great thing.'

Marion didn't know what to say, having thought that any debts were in the reverse order. Ephraim was beaming at her, his dark eyes disappearing in a web of wrinkles.

'We've had a real nice afternoon. What do you say, Patrick?'

'Yes. Indeed.' Not expansive, but adequate. Marion guessed that 'indeed' was a word he had picked up from Mick.

86

'I'm not stopping for a cup of tea, honey. I said I'd meet Walt at four-thirty and I've over-run that now, I think. I'll be back on Wednesday, same time. That okay by you, Patrick?'

'Yes. Fine.'

Ephraim shook hands all round and departed. Pat went out to his car with him, and Ruth poured the tea.

'Splendid! He seems very nice, not a bit stuffy. I always think people who are frightfully good at what they do are going to be stuffy. I don't know why.'

When Pat came back he had Geoff with him.

'I got away early—better than I expected. Not too early, I hope—not very polite, coming to dinner at five.'

'Just what we'd hoped—because we can take Lud and go along the beach first. Get back before he gets too tired and grizzly.'

'I'm tired and grizzly now,' Pat said.

'You need fresh air. What was he like, Ephraim? Did it go all right?'

'Yes. It was pretty good. Fantastic, in fact. Marion's not bad at miracle working. God, I'm exhausted!'

'Here, have a cup of tea. And you, Geoff. I'll go and get Lud ready.'

It was like a holiday, Marion thought, setting out along the beach without any reason at all save to enjoy themselves. She hadn't been on the beach with Geoff since the three of them used to go when Liz was still there, and it was the same now as it had been in those days. Geoff, she realized, had grown very quiet since Liz had died; he hadn't always been such a quiet person. Watching him now, walking with Ruth, with Lud strung between them, it struck her that he was how she could recall him, years back when she was little, laughing and chatting away. She was amazed, having forgotten. She walked behind, on the water's edge, watching, listening. Pat was beside her, abstracted, careless, the incoming waves catching his feet, sloshing over his plimsolls.

'We can go and see the grave,' she said. 'The last grave.' Swithin's grave, she added to herself.

'I'd like to find a bone,' Pat said.

'Daddy's got some bones at home, out of the cliff.'

The sea that had eaten away a whole town looked remarkably innocent, rolling up the gritty sand. Their feet left soft, quaking prints, the sand swelling up round the edges, hardening, the impressions filling with water. Marion could walk along watching her feet without noticing anything else, following the farthest edge of the incoming water. After a bit she noticed that she was wearing her best school sandals, and she stopped to take them off, although it was rather late. The sun shone warmly on the ragged sandy cliffs, the pale wiry grass and humped-up shingle; a small yacht slipped idly along out to sea, the sails scarcely filled, honey-coloured in the evening light. Later, Marion remembered, there would come the loom of the lighthouse and the strange stabs and flickerings of light out at sea as the horizon darkened, the warnings of banks and sands far out. A coaster glittered there now, sparkling white, not looking like anything to do with work at all, more like a decoration, a diamond thrown on a silken sea.

Marion found she was trailing behind, taken up with her feet on the edge of the water. Pat was in front of her, alone, skimming stones to make them bounce; then Ruth waited for him, with Lud, and he took Lud up on his shoulders. Lud took great handfuls of Pat's hair to hold on to and Pat groaned and told him not to, so Lud put his hands over Pat's eyes and Pat started to trip over stones and bits of seaweed with much drama, until Lud was nearly sick with laughing.

'How much farther?' Pat removed Lud's hands, taking in the scenery. 'I'm a sedentary worker, you know. My constitution can't take a lot of this.'

'We're there,' Marion said.

'Where? Where's there?'

'The town that fell in the sea.'

Pat stopped in surprise, the landscape having changed in no way at all, save that the sandy cliffs were fringed with trees, and there were a few boats pulled up the beach and a lane coming down between the trees.

'You mean——?'

'We're standing on it. It's all under the sand and out to sea.'

'There's *nothing* left?'

'No. One grave.'

They caught up with Geoff and Ruth, and Pat put Lud down.

'We're both too old now for me to carry you far. Go and look for bones.'

'This is where I got all mine,' Geoff said. 'Skulls and all. They were two a penny when I was a kid.'

Ruth said, 'Ugh!' looking at the cliffs.

'They used to stick out.'

Marion said to Pat, 'Will you come up and find the grave with me?'

'If you like.'

Geoff and Ruth stayed on the beach with Lud, and Pat followed Marion up to the lane opening. A small beaten track undulated up the sloping, broken cliff-face; the cliffs were not very high, hardly cliffs, and the edge, where the path had originally chosen its route, was broken away in several places. They had to climb and scramble across the deep cuts, until the path turned and ran away from the sea through dense undergrowth and crowded saplings. It was narrow and difficult to get through in places. About fifty yards from the cliff-edge, another even narrower path crossed at right-angles. Marion turned left, back in the direction they had walked from along the beach.

'St. James's Street,' she said. 'They don't bother with traffic lights any more.'

'What do you mean?'

'This path is—was—St. James's Street. The one we were on was the High Street.'

'You're joking?'

'No. I know where everything is—was. We've got all the maps and books on it at home. They belonged to my mother.' She held a vicious encroachment of bramble on one side to stop it springing back on Pat. 'This street runs—ran—to St. James's church, and the inland edge of the graveyard is still there. That's where the grave is. I'll show you.'

They ducked and pushed their way along the peaty track until it ran out on to a clearing of turf and they could see the sea again between mounds of hawthorn and blackberries. They walked on, side by side now. To their right some rocks cropped out of the turf in a curving line.

'That's the old churchyard wall. On the other side there used to be a busy road out of town, going south.'

They stopped for a moment and considered the busy road out of town. Two Red Admiral butterflies spread their gold and brown to the evening sunshine, balancing on a spray of broom, and a bee zoomed on its way, low over the rabbit droppings.

'Swithin lived here,' Marion said softly. 'He must have walked there—right there—every day, out in the morning

and back at night, to work at our church.' She could see his feet printing the dusty road as hers had printed the wet sand, his brown, thoughtful face considering the day's problems on Herbert or Sebastian.

Pat was silent, considering Swithin. If he were to stand on the other side of the stones, and walk south, Marion thought, watching him, and if he had been wearing fustian stuff and leather sandals instead of jeans and plimsolls, he could have been Swithin, the way he looked.

'Our man, you mean? Who carved the angels?'

'Yes.'

Marion led on through some more clumps of bushes and they came to the grave, six feet from the edge of the crumbling sand. Standing there, they could look down on Ruth and Geoff sitting with their backs against one of the fishing boats, talking and throwing stones at a plastic bottle on the water's edge. Lud was looking for bones. They were all too far away to shout to. The sea, violet-blue and hazy, seemed to fill the whole horizon, both very close and very far away, stroking the pink and gold shingle below and the sky beyond. The shadow of the cliff was beginning to creep across the beach with the lowering of the sun, and Marion could see their shadows, hers and Pat's, down below them side by side. Neither of them said anything, looking. Pat sat down on the turf, looking out to sea, resting his back on the grave. Marion sat down beside him. The grave was just a hummock with a curved, body-shaped stone over it, green with moss. Putting her back to it, Marion shivered, thinking of the skeleton below. She was thinking, if it truly was Swithin, it would have a broken leg. If she was an archaeologist, she would get permission to dig it up and see. But by the time she would be old enough to be an archaeologist, it would be gone down the cliff, eaten by the sand and the sea.

She had this feeling again, with Pat, that the silence

92

between them was a mutual acknowledgement of an un-common bond. Or was that the working of her over-active imagination? She felt it, but perhaps he was thinking of the problems set him by Ephraim.

But presently he said, 'This fellow we're leaning against, he won't be here much longer, the way it's going.'

'No.'

'I wonder who he was, what he did?'

'He might be Swithin. Swithin was buried in this corner of the churchyard. The most inland corner. So it might be.'

Pat said, 'I feel at home here.'

Marion thought that a very strange thing to say. It made the hair prickle on the back of her neck. No, she thought. It's the workings of my over-active imagination. Why had he said that?

'What do you mean?'

But he didn't answer.

Instead he said, 'Your father and my wife seem to get on very well together.'

Marion was jolted by the comment. It was given without irony or suspicion, a statement of fact, but Marion was unprepared for the switch. She found it strangely hurtful, she could not say why. She could not say anything, sitting there clasping her knees, staring out at the sea.

'What was your mother like?' Pat asked.

'Like Ruth,' Marion whispered.

Everything Pat was saying was a shock to her system; she felt tuned up for shocks, quivering. But only because of something in herself, more vulnerable than it should have been, not because he was coarse or insensitive. It was being in this place, on this strange ground. She felt wound up, overwound like a watch.

They sat in silence for some time, and Marion felt herself receding. Receding was the word that seemed to explain the

93

feeling, although she knew that a person could not recede. Coming to terms with what had been said, which now, gradually, did not seem shocking at all, merely quite ordinary remarks. Why do I get to feel like that, Marion thought? It's the same as the taking-off feeling, in a slightly different way.

'Why did you say you felt at home here?' she asked Pat, slightly belligerently.

'Did I say that?' He looked surprised. 'I'm ravenous. Let's go back.'

They went back the same way to the beach, and Ruth collected Lud and they all started back, walking together now, Marion and Pat in the water and Geoff and Ruth keeping dry, with Lud between them. Their shadows stretched out to sea; the sea and the sky merged, darkening, and the first light shone far out, faint and green. It seemed farther going back, the sand dragging. Pat and Geoff took it in turns to carry Lud. When they got back to the cottage, Ruth took Lud and Pat, handing him over, walked out into the sea just as he was and swam strongly away into the dusk.

'I'm sorry,' Ruth said. 'He's a lousy host. I thought he'd offer you drinks while I dished up.'

She didn't seem in the least surprised. They all stood watching for a moment, then went back over the dunes to the cottage, into a lovely smell of cooking and the warm tangle of the kitchen, where Geoff got his own beer and Marion supervised Lud's supper and put him to bed while Ruth got their supper ready.

'Look, do you like this?' Ruth, in the middle of setting out the cutlery, reached in to the living-room and brought out a parcel which she threw to Marion. 'If you do, I could make you a dress of that. It's your sort of colour.'

Marion opened it and found a material patterned in blues

94

and violets, rather dusky and muddled, and sprinkled at intervals with small orange flowers. It was rather how the sea had looked from the cliffs, she thought, darkening as the sun left it.

'It's lovely! Will you really?'

'Yes. For going to a concert in? Is that what you want?'

'Long, like yours. Oh, yes!'

'I'll do it this week. I shall enjoy it.'

Geoff looked pleased too. 'That's terribly kind of you. That's just the sort of thing we're not very good at managing —and when you ask other people—'

'Like Mrs. Rowley,' Marion growled.

'—they are very kind, but it never seems to look right, somehow. I know when it looks right, when it's on, but I couldn't for the life of me find it in a shop.'

'I will be your chief adviser,' Ruth said. 'For no charge. I shall enjoy it.' She was laughing, pleased.

When Pat came back, swamping the kitchen, Marion showed him the stuff and told him Ruth was going to make her a concert dress.

'Whose concert? That's the important question.'

'You said—at the dinner—you said—you promised—'

'I didn't promise. I said, if you work at it, perhaps, in the front row at the edge, near the door.'

'I have worked at it. You don't know—' Marion's vehemence caused Geoff to check her.

'Hey, steady on!'

'They are *my* concerts!'

'Marion!' Geoff was furious. Pat was grinning.

'We'll build you a little cage,' he said, 'at the side of the stage. I promise you can come, yes. To the last one. And meantime you can go on practising.'

He went away to get dried and changed and Geoff said to Marion, 'That's not very fair, considering what happened

95

before. I'm not going to let you go if there's any risk of that happening again.'

'I won't let it,' Marion said.

'Well, if you can stop it, that's splendid. It might be the cure, if you want to go badly enough.'

'We could go too,' Ruth said. 'I usually do anyway. I'm sure it will be all right next time. I'm going to dish up. I can't wait any longer.'

The evening was pleasant, Geoff and Pat talking about boats and Ruth, after supper, taking Marion's measurements and going through her patterns for the dress. The men washed up. When it was time to go, Ruth suggested that they come again the following Saturday.

'I'll have the dress ready by then and you can try it on. Come to supper again, then Geoff can still have his day boat-building. I know it would break his heart to miss that.'

Marion couldn't wait for the dress. Geoff was amused.

'I thought you didn't care about clothes?'

'No. Only this clo.' 'Clo' had been her private word, with Liz, for a single garment. 'Anyway, I like going there.'

'Yes, so do I.'

'Why?'

'Why what?'

'Why do you like going there?'

'Because I like them. And you do too, so it all fits. I mean, Horry's wife asks me round for a meal quite often, but it doesn't fit in with you, so I don't bother. If you went there with me, you'd sit and scowl all the evening.'

'I could watch the telly,' Marion said, meek with recognizing the sacrifices Geoff made uncomplainingly for her.

'Don't worry.' He grinned. 'You're quite a good excuse really. But Pat and Ruth are different.'

'Yes.'

By Saturday they had heard from Alfred that the dates of the three concerts had been fixed.

'The one in London is next month. The publicity is all at the printer's already, the advertising booked, Ephraim is appearing on television—quite incredible. A real miracle, one could say.'

'One could indeed!' Geoff said, very polite.

'We at the church end have got to get moving too. I think there will be a lot of visitors. Marion will need some help probably. I'm getting some of the ladies on to it now. I'll try and see that they don't upset Marion—it might be a bit difficult, but try and persuade her that it's all for the church's good, in the end. Some of them are a bit—perhaps, a trifle —bossy, and Marion is apt to—she's—'

'Difficult,' Geoff prompted.

'Yes, a little. She has a way of—well—'

'I know exactly what you mean.'

'Yes. Well. The ladies don't always understand. But I'm sure everyone will work together for the common good. We're going to have signs put on the main road, you know, directing the way to the church, and notices outside about the appeal, a sort of thermometer thing, you know, showing how much we want and how much we've got. You know the sort of thing. Rather vulgar, perhaps, but necessary. And the money-box—I was rather hoping we might rope you in to keep an eye on it. We'll empty it as often as possible, of course.'

'Yes, I'll be glad to.'

'It might all be rather busy down your lane, if things go according to plan.'

It was, relatively, already. Mrs. Rowley came down in her car with three other ladies, all in overalls, with brooms and buckets and scrubbing-brushes. Their husbands, less en-thusiastically, came in the evenings to tidy the graves and the compost heap and instal a privy behind the elder trees, with a notice 'Toilet' nailed discreetly, half-hidden by leaves. Marion was given dire warnings from Geoff to be nice to everyone, and not presume she owned the place.

'You started all this, just remember. You're the one that wants it the most, so don't get temperamental.'

She cleared away the trains and all her things in the priest's room, and the ladies threw out her jamjars full of buttercups and brought back the delphiniums of embarrassing memory, and cut-glass vases of roses six times bigger than any in Marion's garden, without a single caterpillar hole amongst the lot. She had to agree that it all looked rather nice. The church smelled of polish and carbolic. A photographer came and took a lot of photographs. Marion went in in the evenings to see what was different, and remind the angels that it was all due to her.

'You just remember, when you're all fixed, who you've to thank. Who worked the miracle.'

Her friend Flint, denied the train-set, tried to make her help him set it up in his father's workshop instead, but she wouldn't go down to the village. She didn't want to miss anything. Flint's father had bought him a skateboard for his birthday.

'You can have a go on it, if you like. The bit of road down mine is just right, where it's downhill. You need two, anyway, to see if there's anything coming.'

'Bring it up here.'

'It's no good up here. Too much gravel.'

Geoff said, 'I'll buy you a skateboard, if you like.'

'It's no good up here. Too much gravel.'

'You can take it where it's okay.'

'I don't want to.'

'She ought to make friends in the village,' Mrs. Rowley said to Geoff. 'Haven't you ever thought that—' Seeing

Geoff's expression she changed her tack. 'I'm not criticizing, my dear boy. I think you're doing a splendid job. But naturally, it's very difficult for you, out on a limb here, to see that she mixes with the right people.'

'We're going to supper with the Penningtons tonight, as a matter of fact. We often meet Mr. Voigt there.'

'Really!' She couldn't help showing that she was impressed. But she covered up immediately. 'But friends of her own age ... perhaps Melissa and Louise. ...'

'Ugh!' Marion said, on being warned.

'She means well,' Geoff said sharply.

Sometimes he worried that the Mrs. Rowleys of the world were right.

Saturday was hot, and they drove to Fair Winds in the evening amongst all the traffic going home from a day at the seaside. They found Pat changing the oil in his car, and Ruth was putting Lud to bed. Marion went upstairs, and had to read a story to Lud, which was nice, taking her back to the days when Liz had read to her. The memory came back very sharply; even the story was one Liz had read. Everything to do with Ruth, she thought, kept overlapping with her mother. It was strange, for no one else had ever had this effect. Lud was looking extraordinarily clean and cuddly in his cot.

'Can we go and look for bones again?'

'It's a bit late now.'

'I never found one. I want one.'

'I'll bring you one if you like.'

'Oh, yes!'

'Next time.'

Ruth had her dress laid out on her bed, all finished except for the hem.

'Try it on.'

It was every bit as desirable as Marion had hoped. She

stood in front of the mirror, pink with pleasure at her new image, very straight and thin—no, slender was the word—her knobbly knees hidden by the long skirt. Ruth started to pin the hem.

'I wasn't sure if you had a bosom or not. It was a bit tricky.'

'Flattening it?'

'Yes. The pattern was one to fit me. Not that I've got much. But it's come out all right.'

'It's beautiful! Can I keep it on?'

'Why not? Dressed for dinner. Shall I too? We'll give them a surprise!'

She finished the pinning—'I don't think they'll stick in. I'll tack it after dinner'—and changed into one of her dark gipsyish skirts and a tight black shirt. She went to a drawer and pulled out a gold chain which she looped several times round her neck, and a necklace of small rhinestones which she arranged round Marion's neck.

'What do you think?'

'Yes.'

'Just for dinner, special. I can't give it you.'

They went downstairs and got the supper on the table—ham and salad and garlic bread crisp out of the oven—and called Pat and Geoff, who were still doing something to the car.

They came in together, dirty and cheerful, and Marion, standing ready for her father's approval, saw his eyes go straight to Ruth, and an expression in them that, for a moment, shattered her. It was elemental, recognized instinctively, quickly guarded, adjusted.

'Cripes, what is this?' Pat said. 'The Bishop coming again?'

Geoff said to Ruth, 'Marion looks wonderful. You've done a splendid job.'

'Better than that banana gear,' Pat said. 'Very concert-worthy, I would say. Geoff'd better go home for his penguin suit. I'll go up and get my tails.' He sniffed at the marvellous smell of the garlic bread. 'No, hold it, Geoff. It might get cold. We'll come as we are.'

He wiped his hands on the towel hanging on the door and sat down hungrily. Marion watched Geoff cautiously, but everything was quite ordinary again, the moment passed. But she knew that what she had seen was no figment of her over-active imagination. She felt quite thrown by the jar it had given her, moving warily to her place. After the first shock, she realized that it was quite inevitable. She too loved Ruth. Why should it be any different for her father, starved of such a basic emotion for so long?

'What's up? Pin sticking in you?' Pat asked.

'No.' Worse than pins by far. Her miracle was slipping.

'You're practising being quiet and ladylike?'

'Yes.'

'Very good. We might test you after supper.'

'What do you mean?'

'Play to you and see what happens.'

'Really? Do you mean it?'

'We've got to start some time. The first concert is next month, Cambridge and Norwich both quite soon afterwards. You've got to get in training. Ephraim goes back to America in September, as soon as we've done the Norwich gig. The day after, in fact. He suggested I might go with him.'

Ruth, passing the salad, said quietly, 'I trust you declined.'

'I said I'd consider it.'

'Does Mick know?'

'I told him, yes.'

'What did he say? No, don't tell me. I can guess. "A fantastic opportunity!"'

'It's not to play, only to meet a few people, have a holiday. You too.'

'To meet people. To work.'

Pat shrugged. 'Let's not talk about it.'

'No. Let's not.'

The exchange was quick, muted and unexpectedly fierce. Afterwards, when they were talking about cars and boats and normal things, Marion wondered if she had imagined both the fierceness and the look on her father's face. She felt all churned up inside about both things. They were both frightening in their implications. She turned to Pat.

'Did you mean it, about playing to me?'

'If you want me to.'

'Yes, I do.'

'It suits me, to go right through the Chopin studies as if it's for real. I've got to play them in Sheffield on Friday.'

'I thought you were on holiday?'

'Semi.'

Marion was pleased and excited, not having dared to

prompt him about her concert again. When they finished supper, he helped clear away, and Marion dried up while Ruth washed. Ruth said to Geoff, 'You don't want to listen, do you? Do say, not just be polite. We could go for a walk along the beach. Or take some beer out on the dunes.'

'Yes, whatever you wish.'

'We'll go out then. It'll be better practice for Marion.'

She went into the sitting-room and turned a lamp on, and tidied the cushions in the armchair.

'You might be better sitting in the kitchen. You'll find it's very overpowering. The room's so small. In fact, it's best of all out on the dunes. We shall probably enjoy it better out there.'

'No. I shall be all right.' She wanted to watch as well as listen.

'What he's going to play—if you're going to get *sent*, so to speak—it's the sort that will do it. We'll stay if you like.'

'No. It's quite all right.'

'Very well.'

She smiled. 'Enjoy it.'

She went out with Geoff, and Marion sat in the armchair, hugging her knees, waiting. Then she remembered her dress, and sat straight. Pat came in and sat down at the piano. He had put on a clean shirt and tie and looked very serious.

'Opus twenty-five, Chopin,' he said to her. 'I'm not going to stop, you understand.'

'No.'

She felt all shivery and he hadn't played a note yet. He removed some music that was on the rest, and laid the rest down flat, and then sat very still for what seemed to Marion a long time, staring straight ahead of him. Marion clasped her hands together tightly, nervous; for Pat, as she knew him, seemed to have disappeared, exchanged for this remote stranger. When he started to play, rippling very rapid, harp-like notes beneath a lilting, summery melody, she saw again the thing that had set her off before: the expression on his face that had made her think of Swithin carving the angels; she had forgotten it until this minute, this strange transformation, taking on the nature of the music, that she had described to Ruth as 'looking beautiful'; it wasn't really that, although it gave that effect. It was as if he wasn't exactly himself any more, but more a medium through which the music was being expressed.

She hadn't known what to expect this time, and was more nervous because of it, sitting very still in the armchair.

It was all right at first. There was a moth burring under the lamp, and she watched that, it was easier, and the notes whirred like the moth's wings. It galloped, grew louder and more energetic, then launched into a deep, sensuous tune. She looked out of the window, biting her lip, holding herself very still. There were figures on the dunes, outlined against the deep blue sky of the July dusk. She knew now that it was going to be very difficult. She had this very strange feeling that something in the music was moving towards her, that it was going to pick her up and take her with it whether she wanted or not; and in her mind it was the same as her miracle, picking up all these people and driving them along on a path she had not foreseen at all. It was growing all the time more powerful. Sometimes there was a pause, a rest, but too short, and then it would start again, and Pat never once glanced at her or said anything, but was contained in this shell of concentration, forming the music.

It was a mental thing, trying to hold out, and not managing it. The music, first spelling out a very simple tune in single notes, came at her suddenly like a breaking wave, a great torrent of sound, submerging her. The tears streamed down her cheeks. She held on physically, her arms over the sides of the chair and her fingers digging into the upholstery to keep herself from running; but the music would not stop, pouring out in passionate waves that broke and thundered over her. She could not hear herself sobbing for it yet she knew she was, the tears choking her and the miracle running amok, tearing everyone to bits: nothing in her head made sense. She twisted over and turned her face into the cushions, holding her hands over her head, and was still buried there when the music stopped, not aware immediately that it was all over, not until she realized that she was making a terrible noise—it was her, not the music. The cushions were soaked and her hair stuck in wet strands all over her face. She lay there, not daring to come up, all her good intentions in ruins. And she knew Pat was waiting for her.

'Come on,' he said, gently.

She turned her head slightly. Without saying anything else, he started to play again, but this time it was very gentle and pretty, soothing, and she knew he was watching her. It was easier for him to calm her with music than with words. She turned over and came upright, groping for a handkerchief she didn't have. Still playing with one hand, he passed her a clean one out of his pocket.

'Not very good,' he said.

'No.'

'You'll have to do a lot better than that. You'll have to come over more often. Get desensitized. They do it to people who have asthma, with injections.'

'I don't want injections.'

'No. More practice, that's all. Lots of Chopin. Ephraim playing the Franck sonata—staggering. When you can sit through that without boo-hooing, here at home, you can have a free ticket for your concert.'

'Truly?'

'I promise. You've improved a bit already, after all—you

didn't cut and run this time.'

'No. I held on to the armchair.' She looked at her finger-nails and saw that two of them were torn.

'I didn't see what a state you were in till I'd finished. I knew you were still there, that's all.' He stopped playing, the tune having closed away imperceptibly into silence. They both sat there, digesting the strange evening. Marion felt terribly tired.

'I think,' Pat said, 'Chopin would have been quite pleased.'

'With you?'

'With both of us.'

Chapter Seven

Marion broke up, and spent a lot of her time at Fair Winds. Now that it was holiday time, the church was getting a lot of visitors due to Ephraim's publicity scheme, and Mrs. Rowley's gang started to take over. The thermometer bulb painted on the board outside already showed a degree of warmth. Motor coaches started to visit, and the ladies were forever renewing their flower-arrangements and fiddling with the altar. If Marion was around they made her run errands, or—worse—Mrs. Rowley brought Melissa and Louise to play. Marion would get the first bus she could for Fair Winds. After she knew she was welcome there, she went often.

Pat no longer seemed to be on holiday, for he was always working, either with Ephraim or without him.

'Ephraim wants him to go back to America with him afterwards,' Ruth said to Marion. 'I've told him I don't want him to go. It makes him very cross.'

She looked sad, sadder than Marion had ever seen her.

She went on, 'I know I should encourage him, but he works too hard. He doesn't think about anything else at all. After a bit, you begin to wonder what it's all for. Whether it's worth it.'

Marion rather thought it was, being famous and rich.

But Ruth said, 'It's just that there's no room for me and Lud in the programme at all.'

They were sitting on the beach at the time. Ruth rolled over and lay facing up the shingle, looking up towards the dunes, from where the sound of music could faintly be heard on the breeze. Lud was making a castle further down where the sand was. Ruth's fingers moved amongst the stones, picking out the small pink shells and putting them in a pile.

'I ought to make a life of my own, but it's a bit difficult with Lud, and Pat hates me not being around, even when he doesn't say anything for days. But I think, if he goes to America, it will make the break. I shall be on my own for a bit. I shall have to work something out.'

'You won't go?'

'No, I've told him. I've told him he shouldn't go, but if he does, I'm staying. We've had some awful rows about it.'

Marion wished Ruth would stop, not wanting to hear what she was saying, but she went on.

'I know it's a great opportunity and all that, but he's so good that he doesn't need to grasp every opportunity that comes along any more. He can afford to take more time over it. As it is now, he's making plenty of money. It's a good life for him. He gets enough work with orchestras to make him happy, and his recitals are very well attended. If he starts travelling all over the world, then—well—what sort of a life is that? All travelling and hotels and strangers—and he really hates chatting people up and being social—there would be stacks of that—and always a different place for practising . . . all that strain and stress. It's bad enough doing a big concert near home, with me to hold his hand and fend people off—whatever would he feel like in Chicago or New York or somewhere? And I won't go, whatever he says. He doesn't need me, save as a sort of nanny, a servant—he'd be so wrapped up and wound up in the work—' Ruth's voice, which had been gradually rising and getting more indignant, stopped suddenly, and she put her head down into her folded arms and lay very still.

Marion did not know what to say, or do. She had the most dreadful torn-apart feeling inside her, as if she was both Ruth and Pat together, warring over the future. And she felt responsible for what had happened. It had been all right at the beginning, before her prayers. It was Ephraim coming and throwing out this America idea that had sparked it all off. It was why Pat was working so hard and getting so bad-tempered and why Ruth was now lying in transparent misery on the shingle. Lud, trying to make a sand-castle out of a milk-bottle, started to bawl with frustration.

Marion went down to him and explained why it wouldn't work and pointed out how useful it would be instead for getting sea-water for the moat. She emptied the sand out of it, wished there was a solution as straightforward for Ruth. She couldn't bear the thought of Ruth leaving poor Pat to fend for himself. She hated her own part in the business.

When she went home and into the church she decided she hated it smelling of polish and all tarted up with its woman's magaziney flower-arrangements and its beastly thermometer standing on the grass. She hated everything.

'I hate you too,' she said to the angels, staring up at their eternal calm, their peaceful eyeballs watching over the centuries. 'It's all your fault.' She might have guessed, lying in the front pew watching them, as Pat had lain before his concert (did Ruth really need to hold his hand beforehand? He had looked terribly miserable) that miracles were never so simple, that large events conjured out of thin air must inevitably cause repercussions, what doctors called side-effects. She didn't even like the church looking more prosperous and cared-for; she had liked its empty, dusty paleness and its forlorn grandeur humping over the marshes. She didn't like the motor-coaches and the lazy tourists eating their picnics in the churchyard. She didn't want it safe so that it was forever full of tourists and people praying. It wasn't what she wanted at all. She could feel herself getting into one of her states, glaring up at Herbert and Ted who didn't care at all.

'You don't care! All I've done for you and you don't care tuppence! It's all the same to you—Mrs. Rowley and all— you—and Mrs. Rowley and them—'

She got up and started to run, frightening a mild man with binoculars round his neck nearly to death as she sped out of the doorway, shouting, making for home. She crashed into the kitchen, where Geoff was putting a frozen pie in the oven and burst into tears.

'Whatever's the matter?'

'Nothing,' she sobbed, holding herself with her arms, making herself sit still at the kitchen table. Practice with Pat had helped already. Geoff watched her curiously.

'It's a lot of fuss for nothing.'

'Everything then. I just *feel* like it!'

She couldn't tell him, what Ruth had said, what had set her off. Or did he already know? Had they talked about it, sitting on the dunes while Pat had played her into hysterics? She howled.

'Oh, come off it, Marion,' Geoff said, a trifle wearily. 'It can't be just nothing.'

But she couldn't tell him, hung up by the frightening images put forth by her galloping imagination. He was involved too. Her miracle had got him in its web, besides Pat and Ruth.

'Did Ruth say—?' she started, and got no farther, racked by sobs.

Geoff started to peel some potatoes, patient but frowning.

'Ruth rang me up just now. She asked if you and me would go to Fair Winds and baby-sit the night of the London Concert. I said we would.'

'She's got to—to hold Pat's hand—she said—'

'I *beg* your pardon?'

'She said—' Marion made a great effort to get under

control. Her sobs died down to hiccups. 'She has to go—if—if it's a big concert—to—to hold his hand.'

'Metaphorically speaking, I'm sure. Otherwise very difficult for him.'

'Yes.'

Geoff gave her a sideways grin.

'He needs her,' Marion said, hiccuping.

'Does he?' Geoff said, not smiling now.

Marion began to realize then that there was nothing she could do about Pat and Ruth any longer, absolutely nothing at all. Nor Geoff either. Prayers were too dangerous. What good now, to pray that it would come out all right? She saw that it could only come right for some of them, but for all of them, it was impossible. And her father was the most vulnerable of all. But she stopped crying.

They went to baby-sit on the day of the first concert in London. Pat and Ruth were leaving at two in the afternoon, so they arrived in plenty of time. Marion could see that Pat was in the same sort of mood as he had been on the day of the miracle, looking fragile (for him) and pale, and not talking. Ruth was packing his clothes into a suitcase and he was shaving in the bathroom. Ruth looked resigned, and not particularly happy either. Marion felt her responsibilities crowding again.

'You don't mind, do you?'

Ruth looked surprised. 'Mind what?'

'This concert?'

'No. Why ever should I?' She looked puzzled. 'We're never frightfully happy beforehand—well, he isn't, and it rubs off on me rather. But that's quite normal. It's lovely afterwards.'

If that was normal then, Marion felt better.

'It's a big one, this, you see. Lots of musicians will be

there. Harder playing to lots of musicians than just people in out of the rain.'

'They notice all the mistakes?'

'Yes. Harder to please.'

Ruth showed her where everything was, and what there was for tea, and how the television worked, and then she went out to the car with Pat, and they took Lud out to wave good-bye. It seemed to Marion a very glamorous way of life, but when they had gone Geoff said, 'Glad it's not me. Give me computers any day.'

'It makes you rich and famous.'

'Who wants to be rich and famous?'

'Me,' Marion said.

Geoff grinned and said, 'Better start practising then. The piano's right there.'

Marion, out of the blue, framed the question she had been obsessed with for days.

'Do you like Ruth?' She didn't know why she asked it then, or even how she was able to ask it, having wanted to and not dared to for so long. But it came out, unbidden, very sudden.

Geoff said, 'Of course I do.'

'No. You know what I mean—not just *like*—I mean—I mean—'

'Love, you mean.'

'Yes.'

'Yes,' Geoff said. He turned away, but Marion saw his skin flush and darken, the summer-bleached hair paler by contrast, endearingly untidy and needing cutting in a way that made Marion's heart turn over for wanting there to be someone to look after him. *Ruth*! she thought. It was awful, wanting it too, as much as he did.

'But it's not on, so don't think about it,' he said. 'You can see that it's impossible.'

But impossible too not to think about it, now that the words had been said, to think about Ruth being at home, as Liz had been, there all the time. He had thought about it too, she could see.

She—it was only one step farther on—thought about Pat going to America and Ruth staying at home, but it was too treacherous to put into words, something she could not bear to consider.

'It's a pity the way things work out,' Geoff said, putting it with perfect simplicity. 'You can't choose it, as often as not. We want another of your miracles.'

Marion wasn't so sure. She took Lud down on the beach, and it was hot enough to swim, even for Geoff who, for a native, wasn't keen on cold water. Pat swam every day, however cold or rough it was. It was how he worked; he wasn't just a fair-weather man, but took the hard things as well as the easy with a sort of animal stoicism. Marion, making a deep hole with Lud, suddenly remembered the thing he had said the first time they had met in the churchyard, about having been in prison for assaulting somebody. She remembered it with a sense of shock, yet—now she knew him better—it did not seem at all unlikely, for he certainly gave one the impression of having uncommon tensions bottled up inside him. And it struck her, digging the hole, that if he found out that Geoff loved Ruth, he might quite possibly use assault in putting his point of view. Marion had watched enough stories on television to know that it was quite a common reaction; it had also happened in the village; she could recall two instances, without any difficulty. She was quite sure that he wouldn't like the idea of Geoff loving Ruth. Ruth said Pat didn't need her, but Marion was quite sure that he needed her badly by his own lights.

'You're diggin' *my* hole,' Lud said crossly, and hit her on the head with his spade.

'You beast!' He was just like Pat, standing there scowling, underlip thrust out, all ready for another assault. 'You mustn't hit people, even if they annoy you!' She thought of adding, 'Your daddy was put in prison for it,' but didn't. She said, 'I'm going to dig one big enough to put you in. Would you like that?'

'Will you bury me?'

'Yes.'

'Yes. Bury me.'

Marion was glad to get on with her digging, having made herself miserable with her thoughts and not being able to convince herself that it was mere imagination. She tried resolutely not to think about any of the things that worried her, but it was difficult. Geoff didn't help by getting bored and rather irritable, and it struck Marion afresh that baby-sitting was what he had been doing for the last five years,

ever since Liz had died. He had never gone out in the evenings or gone sailing at week-ends with Horry or fishing with Ted as she could remember him doing way back when she was little. She had heard it said, in fact, that as a young man he had been rather wild—hence herself. Yet one would never suspect it now. When they had put Lud to bed in the

evening they couldn't even go for a walk. She had never realized before just how very confining the whole business of having babies could be. She wondered if Geoff ever wished he hadn't got her? She was sure now that he did, but wasn't going to ask. She went to bed subdued and miserable.

She didn't know what time Pat and Ruth came home, save that there was a pearly light outside, not dark enough for still being night, yet hardly day. They came up quietly enough, but Marion was restless. She was on a spare bed in Lud's room (Geoff was on the sofa downstairs) and her bed was against the partition wall between the two bedrooms. She didn't want to eavesdrop, but however hard she tried to disassociate her mind from next-door she could not help but realize that the soft, urgent conversation was definitely an argument. It was vicious on Pat's side and equally fierce on Ruth's and hissed backwards and forwards across the bedroom as they undressed and continued after the light had been put out. Marion, unwillingly, caught odd phrases: 'I was a fool to think, when I married you, that anything would change—' countered by, angrily, 'But you knew, you always knew, even then—I *told* you!' 'My mother told me!' Ruth sobbed.

Marion put her head under the blankets and squashed the pillow down over her ears. She was shivering, miserable enough to die of it, she felt.

In the morning Pat stayed in bed and Ruth was in the kitchen, dark rings of weariness under her eyes, putting Lud in his high chair for his breakfast. Geoff came in cheerfully from the living-room, pulling a jersey on. Marion stood in the doorway, white and silent.

'Hullo,' Ruth said brightly. 'Was everything okay?'

'Fine,' Geoff said.

'I hope we didn't wake you, coming home? We were pretty late.'

'Never heard a sound. Your sofa's very comfortable. What's the matter with you, Marion? You look like a wet week.'

'Nothing,' Marion said, amazed by adult machinations.

'Did it go well?' Geoff asked.

'Yes. Absolutely splendid. They had to do three encores —wonderful reception. It should get a very good press.'

'Pat having the day in bed on the strength of it?'

Ruth frowned momentarily. 'He was tired, yes.'

They stayed for breakfast, and drove home. Marion was silent, wondering if it all mattered as much as she thought it did. Geoff was quiet too, abstracted. Neither of them remarked on the common mood, and when they got home Geoff went down to work on his boat and Marion went to top up the flower-vases in the church. There were a lot of visitors that day, and she did her guide job, and watched the money rattling into the thermometer box. Geoff had to count it, and move the needle up the temperature chart.

'Seems to be working, your miracle,' he said.

Marion went to Fair Winds a few days later and found everything apparently normal, Pat working and Ruth quite cheerful.

Pat, emerging for lunch, said he had a ticket for her for the Norwich concert.

'Front row, easy for rapid exit if necessary.'

'Is Ruth coming?'

'No,' Ruth said.

'You'll be on your own,' Pat said. 'You can come with me. I'll look after you.'

'And bring me back?' Marion was hesitant, because of his going to America the day after.

'Yes. I'm coming back here for a few hours' kip, then down to Heathrow first thing in the morning.'

Marion glanced at Ruth, but she looked quite calm and

non-committal. Perhaps everything had been worked out amicably after all, Marion thought? She was asking Pat about arrangements for the following day.

'You've got Newcastle tomorrow night?'

'And York the day after, so I'll stay up there, drive home as soon as I've finished.'

'I'll put two shirts in then, and your night things.'

'Yes.'

All very wifely and even-tempered. Pat drove north, and Ruth asked Marion to baby-sit for her the evening he was away. She did so, thinking nothing of it.

The following day, Saturday, she was in the church to tidy up for the week-end visitors when the scorned Melissa Rowley arrived with a bunch of her mother's fresh flowers to get ready for the weekly flower arranging. Marion usually got the job of washing out the smelly vases at the tap down by the rubbish-tip and clearing up the debris, and made to disappear, but Melissa and her friend Louise offered her some liquorice allsorts. They were giggling and nudging each other.

'You can have the coconut one if you like.'

'I like the ones with beads on best.'

'All right. You can have them both.'

Marion fished her fingers into the box.

'My father saw yours last night,' Louise said, grinning. 'He said he's courting. Did you know?'

Marion concentrated on the blue liquorice allsorts, not looking up. She felt great flames engulfing her.

'He's not!'

'Truly, having dinner at the Goat and Compass. Gazing into her eyes. My father said.'

'Well, and if he is, she's *beautiful*! She's not a great fat cow like your mother! She's not—'

'She's *married*—'

Marion kicked Louise, hard, on the shin, and she buckled up with a squeal, showering liquorice allsorts. Marion ran, as she had run on the day of the concert, desperate for sanctuary, all her squashed-down fears bursting out into the old familiar wildness, uncontainable. Mrs. Rowley, coming in at the door with greenhouse chrysanthemums as big as footballs, staggered as the cyclone passed by. The great latch on the door crashed, echoing all round the roof like a peal on the organ bass notes. Marion ran, and knew there was no one to go to; she was on her own.

She made for the elder trees and the cave of long, burnt grass where the mowers hadn't bothered, filled with the rank smell of the faded blossoms, where she had watched Pat from after the concert. She crouched there, holding her arms round herself, knowing that Louise had been speaking the truth, that her father was courting Ruth while Pat was away, and that if Pat went to America—'Oh, Ruth! Ruth! I do want you too,' she wept. 'But it isn't *fair*! It isn't fair!' She cried herself sick, silently, shaking.

One of the husbands came and started the motor mower, and she could see the grass whirling in its wake and smell the crushed, damp smell. Everyone was going on in their Saturday morning way, even Geoff on the boat, and Ruth, no doubt, on the beach with Lud, and nothing was any different, but she felt as if her angels had fallen.

She emerged an hour later when the coast was clear, damp and crushed as the mown grass, but having surfaced without help, older, wiser, sick with foreboding. She went and made toasted cheese, and called Geoff up from the boat. He came in, whistling, and washed his hands in the sink. He smelled terribly of glue.

'I got something in my eye,' Marion said, as he stared at her across the table. She could deceive as well as anybody if she had to.

'Baby elephant by the look of you.'

'It's all right now.'

'Good.'

'Is Pat still going to America?'

'Yes, I think so. Why?'

'I just wondered. Ruth doesn't want him to.'

'I know. It's difficult.' He said it lightly, eating toasted cheese.

'If he goes—' She was going to say, will Ruth come to you here? But she knew she couldn't ask. She wasn't quite sure how it worked, this divorce thing, people changing over when they were married. And anyway, although she knew her father loved Ruth, she didn't know if Ruth loved her father. But if Ruth was just left alone, without Pat, it seemed very likely that. . . .

She started again. 'Will Pat be away long?'

'No, not this time. I think the idea is to plan an American tour for next year some time. It will be quite a long time then. That's what Ruth doesn't want, for him to do long tours abroad.'

'But that means he's successful, if they want him?'

'Exactly. She should be pleased, and she knows that, and it makes her feel worse that she can't enjoy his being successful. Because it takes him away from her.'

'She *loves* him?' Marion asked fiercely.

'Yes, if she didn't she wouldn't care, would she?'

It wasn't like she thought then! Marion felt a great lurch of relief, uncertainty. . . .

'But—'

'The trouble is,' Geoff said steadily, 'it's a very unsatisfactory life for her, loving someone who either isn't there or, when he is, is so wrapped up in his work that he hardly notices her. So Pat's going to America is a sort of decision-making thing. She's got to decide what's best to do. If he goes away she thinks she'll be able to make up her mind one way or another.'

'And if he decides not to go?'

'Well, I think he's decided. But if he doesn't, I suppose it might all be O.K.—for the time being. It's a bit of a test, in a way, of what he wants most, his work or her.'

It really was, then, as bad as she had thought. Her miracle had brought the whole thing about; without Ephraim it would never have happened. She mumbled this to Geoff, pushing away her plate, tears pricking again.

But Geoff said gently, 'No, Marion. Sooner or later it would have happened. Ephraim's offer just makes it sooner.'

But Marion didn't agree. Later, when Pat and Ruth were back in London, and Geoff was no longer there for Ruth to turn to, everything would be all right. At least, as all right as before the miracle.

Worst of all, worse than anything else, the thing she wanted most in the whole world was for Ruth to come here to live with her and Geoff. She put her arms on the table, buried her head in them and cried.

Chapter Eight

'Hullo, Marion. Did you get blown all the way here?'

Ruth opened the door and let Marion in, along with a blast of wind and a skirling of sand. It was as if, on the day of the Norwich concert, the day before Pat's departure for America, God had decided to add suitable atmospherics, for the weather was as thundery as the mood at Fair Winds. Foul Winds more like, Marion thought, seeing the bleakness in Ruth's face. A large suitcase with fresh Pan-Am airline labels stood ready packed. A smaller one lay on the table, into which Ruth was folding Pat's concert clothes.

'Is he really going tomorrow?' Marion asked.

'Yes.'

No respite then. Marion shivered.

'Marion's here, Pat,' Ruth called towards the living-room door. Pat was sitting at the piano studying some music, but did not respond.

'I should warn you,' Ruth said softly to Marion, 'he's horrible before a concert. Don't expect too much. Afterwards he'll be all right. It's nerves.'

Marion was amazed. Her face showed it, for Ruth smiled and said, 'Don't worry. You're not nervous about—about— you know—?'

'No, I won't. I promised.'

She was terribly nervous about it, but Pat had said she could beat it if she tried, and she had improved enormously. He was her living proof, having grown out of beating up people who annoyed him. She would sit like a statue all through the concert, as if nailed to her seat, and any tears would be silent ones. It was for Pat: she was determined not to disgrace him. It was her great test. In her own way, she was as nervous as Pat.

Pat came out of the living-room and put some music in the case.

'Hi, Marion. You all fit to go?'

'Yes.'

He glanced at his watch. He was pale and scowling. Out of the window behind him the sea was lashing up the beach, dark under low, bruised clouds. It was half-past five, but looked three hours later.

'O.K. then, we'll get moving.'

He shut the case and swung it off the table, and took his car keys off the dresser. Ruth came to the door with them, but he didn't say anything to her. Marion wanted to say something nice, to cheer her up, but nothing came to mind and she followed Pat dumbly out to the car and got in. He flung his case in the back, got in and they roared away down the road towards civilization. It was so dark he had to put the lights on. Marion could feel the buffeting of the wind, and splatters of wild rain threshed the windows, but Pat drove fast, heedless.

'What time is your plane tomorrow?' Marion asked him.

'Eleven o'clock.'

'You'll have to leave very early.'

'Yes, I will.'

Marion wanted to say, 'Don't go,' but knew she couldn't. Pat was still scowling, closed-up, concentrating on the road. He was like a stranger. Marion presumed this was what Ruth meant by 'being horrible'. Perhaps best not to talk, but just stare out at the familiar landscape, unfamiliar under the dark weather, pale fields of stubble ghostly under the purple sky, a church tower gleaming, cows turning their backs. She was nervous too, looking for reassurance. But there wasn't any. Presumably for Pat neither, until it was all over.

They came into Norwich, not a word having been exchanged all the way. Pat parked the car. There was a theatre with a lot of posters for the concert, but the doors were still locked. Pat went round the back to the stage-door, and there was someone there to let them in and put the lights on.

'Can I have the stage lights on?' Pat asked.

'You want to try the piano? The tuner only left an hour ago.'

The lights came on and revealed the enormous black concert grand like a recumbent lion bathed in light, and the cavernous maw of the auditorium beyond. Marion, curious, went out on the stage and thought of being a performer exposed to this quixotic gloom, and didn't think she would like it: enough to merely sample it empty. It was unnerving. But perhaps, when he was playing, he never noticed. Only at the beginning, when he had admitted that it was nasty, the getting started.

He played what sounded to Marion like scales for twenty minutes, then the stage-manager came and told him the doors would be opening very shortly, and he stopped and went back to the dressing-room. Ephraim and Mick were there. Ephraim was in evening dress, playing his violin, and Mick was in an armchair reading a stage magazine.

'Why, my little agent! Patrick! You didn't tell me we were having such an important visitor tonight!' Ephraim put his bow arm round Marion and kissed her cheek. He wasn't much taller than she was.

Marion noticed that Mick didn't look quite so pleased, and suspected that he was remembering the St. Michael's concert. He got up though, and gave her a kiss too. He smelled lovely. Marion didn't know what to say.

Pat opened his suitcase and shook out his concert clothes. The transformation, out of the habitual jeans and pullover into the white shirt and waistcoat and black tail suit, staggered Marion. The ticket for her seat was folded into the white handkerchief that Ruth had dutifully supplied, and he gave it to her, speaking to her for the first time since the short exchange at the beginning of the car journey.

'You'll be all right. I know you will.' And he actually smiled.

'I'll take her down now,' Mick said.

'Enjoy it, my little pigeon,' Ephraim said.

'Thank you.' One didn't say 'good luck' to Ephraim Voigt, she felt sure, but to Pat it was surely not out of place, this concert counting as one of the ones that mattered a lot? She whispered it to him, following Mick to the door, and he gave her a bleak look and said, 'And you too.'

The seat in the front row had a good wide gangway in front of it and the Exit door was close at hand. Mick looked relieved, shepherding her through the throng.

'You'll be all right on your own? I've got to go back—I

might have to turn over for Pat, unless they produce someone.'

'Yes.'

He still looked anxious, but Marion smiled at him. She wasn't afraid, no more than Pat.

It was a help, in a way, knowing how he felt, and seeing how he transcended it: the example before her very eyes. She wasn't going to give way this time, however the music might move her. A part of her was holding back, very conscious of the responsibility, and if it meant that she wasn't entirely free to involve her senses with the beautiful music, it also meant that she was less likely to disgrace herself. It was like being under the elder bush in the churchyard, and knowing that she was on her own, with no Geoff there to field her. It just had to work; there was no alternative. And as Ephraim's violin soared above the piano's outpouring she found her arms crossing over and holding the opposite seat-arms hard, and knew the tears were falling down her cheeks, but knew too that she was all in hand in spite of it, silent and contained, triumphant.

At the end of the César Franck when Pat took his bow he looked for her. Marion, clapping madly, saw him smile, and thought he winked. They had to play several encores. The house was in an uproar of applause, and Marion cried again, but only at the end when everyone was getting up and groping for their coats did she let herself go, leaping out of her seat and making for the back of the stage. She felt electrified in her release, not aware until she got up of how much the effort had cost her. She blundered through swing doors, saw Pat in the wings talking amongst a group of people and went to him like a moth to a candle. To her intense relief he took her, unembarrassed, and put his arm round her while she buried her face in the front of his beautiful tailcoat. She wasn't exactly crying, more like getting herself straight, her

126

breath coming in shivering gasps, but improving. He took out his large white handkerchief and gave it her to cover up with.

'Did you like it that much, idiot child? Is that how good it was?'

'Yes!'

'I told you you could do it.'

He took her back to the dressing-room, still with his arm round her, and sat her down in the armchair.

'Don't spoil it now.'

'No.'

He was grinning, the old, nice Pat, nothing like the cold stranger in the car. Looking at him, thinking of him going to America in the morning nearly made her cry again, but she shied her thoughts away fiercely.

'I'm sorry. I'm sorry.'

'No. It's splendid. You managed beautifully. Geoff will be pleased.'

The room seemed to be full of people talking but no one took any notice of Marion, which pleased her. When it thinned out a bit Pat changed back into his old clothes.

'I'm not going to hang around. I want to get back,' he said to Mick. 'There's not much time now.'

'No. Ephraim too. I'll see you in the departure lounge then. No later than ten thirty.'

'Yes.'

'Mind how you go. There's a storm blowing outside.'

Ephraim came and embraced Marion again, to say good-bye.

'Thanks to you, this has been a real fine holiday. I sure have enjoyed giving these concerts and meeting all these fine people.'

'Thank *you*, for the church.'

'It's been my pleasure, believe me!'

They left the theatre, head down into a gale of wind, Ephraim clutching his violin case in both hands. His chauffeur was outside with the enormous car, opening the door ready. Final good-byes were shredded by the wind. Pat and Marion butted their way back to Pat's two-seater and ducked in. It was a relief to slam the doors.

'What a night! Lucky we're close to the ground in this job.'

Once out of the city boundaries the roads were dark, empty and wild. Pat drove very fast, the powerful headlights searing convulsed hedgerows and flailing trees. Leaves came at them like snowflakes. Sometimes the car shuddered, and Pat's hands would tighten on the wheel.

'Are you tired?' he asked her.

'No.'

She felt strangely exhilarated, as if infected by the weather.

Pat said, 'I shan't sleep tonight.'

'You shouldn't go,' Marion said fiercely, suddenly.

Pat frowned, surprised, and said, 'Why do you say that?'

'Because of Ruth.'

'She ought to come. I want her to. I need her.'

'She says you don't need her.'

'She's wrong.'

'The work matters to you more than she does.'

'The work matters very much, but not more nor less than Ruth. You can't measure it.'

Marion didn't say anything else, wondering what had possessed her to broach the subject at all, and after a few minutes Pat said, 'Has she spoken to you about it?'

'A little bit.'

'Has she spoken to Geoff?'

'I don't know.'

'I think so. She and Geoff—'

He did not finish the sentence. Marion looked at him,

feeling her pulses beating uncomfortably, but he was watching the road. His face was very strained and alight, not relaxed at all. He didn't look as if he was going to sleep that night or ever again.

'Nothing is any different now from how it's been all along, right from the beginning. She knew. I can't change it. She thinks I don't need her. I can't make her think otherwise. I know it's hard for her, but I told her—I told her—' He stopped, blinking at a flash of lightning that suddenly split the horizon ahead of them. The road was momentarily white, dazzling, dancing with rain. Marion winced, waiting for the thunder. But Pat laughed.

'Your magic's at work again, Marion—we're going to part in a flash of lightning. The way I feel now, it's exactly right. Thunder and lightning all the way.'

The speedometer was just under seventy, the road glittering and the sky fragmented with sheet lightning.

'It is because of my miracle, in a way,' Marion said, agonized.

'Yes. You'll have to work another to solve this one.'

'But it was for the *angels*! It wasn't supposed to be about people at all.'

'Everything's about people, in the end.'

Marion thought about this, hurtling eastwards and feeling that life was never going to be quite the same again. She knew that she was on the verge of one of her states, but that Pat was the same too, strung up to a condition of rare perception. At least, it felt like rare perception but perhaps that was only an illusion: how could one tell? The emotions of the evening and of the impending departure, spurred by nature's extraordinary intervention, combined to put everything into heightened perspective. But whether that was reality . . . ? Marion was adrift.

They sped down the main road beside the marshes, bearing

inland for Marion's village. Marion could not contemplate the thought of saying good-bye and what was going to happen. They truly did need another miracle, she thought. Or never to have had one.

'What are you going to do?' she asked tightly.

'I can't go to Ruth now, not to all that agony. I shall just put my hand round the door, collect my case and go.' He throttled down sharply for the turning to the church. 'Is Geoff waiting up for you?' The light was on in the cottage. 'I'm not stopping. Tell Geoff good-bye for me.'

'Yes.'

Marion opened the door of the car, holding it against the wind. It was harder now to control her feelings than it had ever been. She could not open her mouth to say good-bye and thank you and all the proper things, because she knew it would come out in sobs and confusion. She had to bite her lip very hard to stop it. She could not bear even to look at him, knowing now that he was no longer watching the road but watching her. She shook her head blindly, slammed the door and ran. She didn't have to use much energy, for the wind took her like a discarded bus ticket and whirled her across the lane. A flash of lightning simultaneously lit the church tower, white and quivering against the electric sky. She dived for the door, and Geoff came to her frenzied knocking.

'God, what a night! I was worried!'

The wind blew her into the kitchen and Geoff put his shoulder to the door to shut it, stopping to put the bolts in and the doormat over the draughts at the bottom. Marion locked herself in the lavatory to get herself into a semblance of normal, and came out when Geoff called, 'Fallen down the plug-hole? I want to go to bed.'

'How was it?' He had made a cup of tea, and was pouring it out for her. A dying fire glowed in the old kitchen fireplace. Marion was shivering although she wasn't cold.

'It was lovely. I was all right—everything was all right.'

She didn't want him to be curious. Nothing was all right, but she didn't want him to know.

'I was a bit worried about the drive home—the roads wet. I've seen how Pat drives, and he would be tired after that. It's a terrible night.' He yawned. 'Glad you were O.K. That's what matters really.'

'Yes.' She mustn't spoil it.

She drank the tea as fast as she could. He was waiting for her, ready to put the lights out. She went upstairs and undressed, and got into bed. She knew she wasn't going to go to sleep, but when her father said good-night she replied in a sleepy voice. She heard him get into bed next door. The lightning trembled outside, pink and hypnotic.

Falling asleep would have solved everything. But Marion knew it wasn't going to happen. Not for Pat either, she felt sure. What was he doing? If he didn't go to bed, there was a lot of time to fill in between now, midnight, and being at Heathrow at half-past ten. Was he going to drive his car all night down the slashing wet roads, working out his salvation? Ruth had told her that sometimes, after concerts, he went out driving because he couldn't sleep, and would stay out until dawn. Not always. But tonight, Marion thought . . . yes . . . she could picture him arriving home, creeping into the kitchen to get his suitcase for America, and taking it out to the car. She opened her eyes as the lightning ricocheted round her bedroom walls, and in her mind saw the same lightning flaring across the beach at Fair Winds, and the black sea crashing beyond the dunes, the spray whipped in streamers. She saw Pat standing on the dunes, watching, his hair flying out . . . he *would*, she thought, yes—but don't go swimming, she said out loud, knowing that it would pass through his mind, the sort of thing that would appeal . . . *no!*

He would have more sense than that, tonight, although she knew he liked swimming in rough seas; she had seen him at it, and watched him come in, laughing and gasping. But tonight it would eat him up, the waves would fold him over and grind him on the stony bottom and lift him up like a plastic bottle.... She got out of bed and went to the window and saw the church very close, like a white cliff, every flint and crenellation etched fine in the flickering storm, the tower trembling; could feel the angels wide-stretched to the howling of the wind outside, quivering on their rusted bolts. She went out of her bedroom to the bathroom, to see the view to seaward, moving very quietly, avoiding the squeaks. The snaking river, full to the brim, gleamed in silver loops to the far horizon and the loom of the lighthouse was dim in competition, feebly revolving. The marsh reeds were laid flat. The tide was high and scouring the land. Farther north, beyond Oldbridge, the cliffs would be tormented by the power of the waves, clinging to the roots of the saplings and the matt of the turf. The grave.... Marion started to cry.

She went back to bed and tried not to think about it. She buried her face in the pillow. But she *knew*....

Was she awake, bound hysterically by the workings of her over-active imagination, or was she really asleep, dreaming that she saw it so clearly: Pat walking off his worries in the eye of the storm, leaning against the wind on the cliff edge with the auditorium of the heaving sea stretched to heaven on all sides and the turf quivering beneath him, the last bones stirring in the soil, the soil loosening, the cliff slipping....

Marion got out of bed again. It was too much. It needed another miracle to get them out of this, and there was only one place now to find peace. She wasn't mad, she knew it—proved it by pulling on her jeans and jersey and fastening her sandals. She went downstairs and out of the back door where it was sheltered from the wind, and ran for the church. It was magnificent, the wind tearing her, the building rocking against the sky above her. She opened the door and ran up the aisle. The whole place was bathed in white light and the angels' wings flashed and flickered against the arched roof. She stood on the altar steps and looked down the body of the church, lifting up her arms and ready to pray. The angels were watching her; she looked up and saw Herbert, the least angelic, his sardonic smile fixed in pity.

'Pray properly, girl, on your knees!' he was saying, and she dropped her arms, went to the front pew and fell on her knees. It was perfectly simple then.

'Please God, make it all come right.'

It was very strange, but it was as if the whole church was moving. There was a rumbling noise, not like thunder, although it was in the sky and moving, coming closer. She straightened up and looked up at the roof. The roof was moving. The angels had taken off and were coming towards her, great wings outspread as if in protection. She saw Herbert gliding, no longer fixed to the roof, saw him coming down as if to enfold her, his smile more tender than she remembered, ducked her head because of the noise which seemed, somehow, to have arrived.

And knew no more.

Chapter Nine

Geoff was awoken in the middle of the night by knocking on the door. He got up and put his head out of the window.

'Who is it?'

'It's me—Pat—'

'Wait a minute.'

He went down, shaking himself awake, not entirely amazed, knowing Pat—more curious.

Pat was already inside, leaning against the door. He was soaked through, grinning.

'Guess what—I thought you ought to know—your church tower has blown down.'

Geoff didn't take it in immediately.

'What did you say?'

'The church—go and take a look. All my work in vain. The whole bloody roof caved in and you still fast asleep in your bed!'

'You're joking—'

'At three o'clock in the morning?'

Geoff went out in his pyjamas. Coming round the side of the cottage into the blast of the wind he saw the extraordinary sight of St. Michael's with only half a tower. With the sheet lightning still flickering round the sky, he could also see the hole in the roof caused by the falling stone, large enough to drop a bulldozer through.

'Christ!'

'And you slept through it—'

'And Marion. Her room faces it—Christ, it's uncanny—tonight—'

'You don't get storms like this every day of the week.

134

Whole cliffs have fallen apart up the coast.'

'What am I supposed to do, for God's sake?'

'Nothing, till morning. If you ring up the vicar he can't do anything. Poor old Ephraim!'

They went back indoors. Geoff rubbed back his hair, scowling. 'I always sleep like a log. I waited up for Marion— Christ, what timing—right after your bloody concert to shore the old place up! What the hell are you doing anyway? You're supposed to be going to America in the morning?'

'Yes, well—I felt all steamed up after the concert. Couldn't face going back to Ruth—bit of a mess, really, with her ... I went along the cliffs. I feel like that sometimes, after a big do. Can't sleep. I go driving or something. Well, I saw it go, from the cliffs, in a flash of lightning. It was fantastic, right across the valley, as sharp as daylight, the whole top just rolled off.'

'The cliffs beyond Oldbridge? But that's three miles away—'

'Yes. But it sticks up like an aeroplane hangar from across the marshes, you know it does. And the light was extra-ordinary. It was really weird—the whole thing, standing up there in the storm and the sea thundering up the beach. I felt like God.' He laughed. 'I felt like a conductor.'

'And I slept through it! Marion too, else she'd be having hysterics by now. Poor kid, when she sees it!'

'Yes, and old Ephraim. He'll be sick. All that money we've been producing—it'll need that just to fill that hole in, by the look of it.'

'I feel we ought to do something about it really. Don't know what though, till morning. Perhaps we should go and assess the damage? Might be a bit dangerous though. Or ought you to get some sleep in, if you've got to drive to London? You can have my bed if you like.'

'No, I won't sleep. I can take some pills to keep me on my

feet till Heathrow, sleep on the plane. Let's go and look at the damage.'

'I'll go and get some clothes on.'

Geoff went upstairs, got dressed, put his head round Marion's door.

He came down, frowning.

'Marion's bed's empty.'

'Perhaps it did wake her then—must have! She's probably out there now.'

'Oh, Lord—complications. It'll send her off the deep end when she sees this. Let's go and find her.'

They went out and across the lane, Geoff apprehensive. They circled the tower and decided that the bottom two-thirds which remained standing looked in no danger of imminent collapse. There was no sign of Marion, but the door was open. They went in, Geoff feeling distinctly uneasy.

'Marion!' he shouted.

The night sky, glittering with stars, spread a strange light overhead where normally the angels flew against darkness. The wind soughed through, skirling in the flowers and the Mother's Union banners, bowling some leaflets down the nave and a few loose hymn-book pages, moaning in the trunk of the tower. At the top end of the nave, across the front pews and the lectern, a great pile of rubble blocked the way to the altar. Worm-riddled timbers, split across, stuck out like the spars of a wrecked ship. A great pile of crumbled bricks, stones and mortar humped across the flags and splintered pews, the mortar dust lying thick over everything and still heavy in the cold air, clamming the throat.

'Jesus!' Pat said, staring.

Two of the angels had disappeared, presumably under the debris, one had fallen across the altar and one into the choir stalls, two more swayed precariously from the sagging roof beyond the hole and the remaining six were still safely in place.

Even Geoff, having taken the church for granted all his life, never actively appreciating, felt crushed by the scene, and not entirely on Marion's behalf.

'Where is she?' he muttered angrily. 'It's not too safe in here. She ought to have more sense.'

He looked under the tower and in the Priest's room and went out in the churchyard to her hole under the elder-trees and back to the house. He noticed that her clothes were missing, and her sandals. He went back to the church, trying to hold down his fear.

'The door was open,' he said to Pat, 'when we came in. You noticed?'

'Yes, but the blast of the roof falling might have done that.'

'What, with that latch? I doubt it. It weighs a ton.'

'Oh, cripes, you're not thinking—?'

'I think I am,' Geoff said quietly. 'Yes.'

They stood side by side, looking. The wind soughed overhead, the sky pale and brilliant, the storm receding. The disturbed angels swayed and creaked. Soft rain came through the hole, spiking silently into the mortar carpet. There was the smell of the river with it, and the coldness of dawn.

They walked down to the pile of rubble, their feet crunching in the dust, and stood looking at it.

'She always goes to the front pew. This one, under the lectern.'

The stones and rubble covering it were as high as their heads.

'But I don't see why—tonight . . .'

'She mentioned another miracle,' Pat said. 'I said we needed one. You don't think she might have—? Oh, Christ! She was strung up when she left me. We both were.'

'We'll have another hunt round,' Geoff said, desperate.

137

But she was nowhere, the house empty, the river banks silent.

'We'll have to look, to dig,' Geoff said. 'There's nothing else to think. *I* will—you, oh God, you've got to get off, haven't you?'

'No. I'll help you. Is there anyone else?'

'They're all a hundred and ten down here, except Marion and me. I suppose I ought to ring the police.'

The phone was out of order, the telephone lines torn down by the wind. Geoff was frantic. 'Let's start. If it's hopeless, we'll drive out for help, but it'll waste time—I mean, we might be wasting time now, if she's—she's—'

He got some tools. Pat scooped his driving gloves out of his car. 'Look, it's stupid not to go for help. I can drive—'

'It'll be half an hour, there and back, if the phone's out.'

'I'll go and tell someone else to go, and come back.'

'Go to the shop on the corner then. Tell George. He's got a car. Tell him to go for the police, the fire brigade or whatever.'

Pat roared up the lane and thundered on the shop door. A man put his head out of the window and got the message, his face sagging with amazement. Pat went back to the church where Geoff was already at work, pulled on his gloves and joined him. It was better, he realized: something in one's terrible anxiety lent itself to attacking bricks and stones, hurling them aside, aiming to free the open end of the front pew.

There was nothing to say, no help in voicing thoughts, no breath to waste, in fact. Even when the police came they didn't stop. Geoff answered their questions over his shoulder, deep in the slithering pile, hurling the rubble out behind him like a terrier. Pat was beside him, only head and shoulders showing.

'I think we want more manpower,' the police decided, and

drove out for reinforcements. By the time daylight was filtering in through the hole above them the work party was considerable and there was much coming and going. Pat uncovered the broken poppyhead of the end pew.

'Look,' he said to Geoff. 'We've arrived.'

They leaned back momentarily in their corridor of debris and in the cold daylight exchanged glances.

'You want a break in there?' someone shouted behind them.

'No.'

There was a plank of heavy, rough-hewn oak jutting out just beyond the poppyhead. Pat reached out for it experimentally.

'It's one of the bloody angels,' he said to Geoff.

The thought of Marion being killed by one of her angels was too dire to voice. Geoff's face was as ashen as the plaster dust that covered it.

'Let's clear it.'

Volunteers started to work from the other side, unburying the angel, which was face upwards. The church had filled up by now with village people, but Geoff and Pat were wedged in the pew opening, invisible to most of the crowd, and working together with an instinct for what might win, and what wouldn't.

'There's a gap—'

'The angel's made a bridge.'

'Pass it to me—carefully.'

Pat had found an opening beneath the angel's wing. It was space beyond, not rubble. He handed the stones back, widening the gap, fearful of sending an avalanche down inside. Gradually they made an opening. There was only room for the two of them to work.

'If they pass us a torch—'

'Oh, Jesus, I don't want to know,' Geoff said.

'There's a chance, with the angel, don't you see? Hold on.'
The message went back and a torch was handed through.
An ambulance had arrived, and ambulance men hovered at
the brink of the rubble.

Pat took the torch and peered into the hole. Geoff watched
his face, what he could see of it for grime. He saw the
expression, and knew.

'She's there!'

'Yes.'

Silence.

Geoff could see it in Pat's face. Pat wriggled back and put an arm round his shoulders, gave him the torch.

'Look for yourself. It's as if she's asleep.'

Beneath the angel's wings, supported by the heavy timber of the old pew, there was a tiny cave where the stones hadn't encroached. The torchlight showed Marion's body lying, covered with white dust, looking as if made of alabaster. There was a roof timber across her legs and beyond it a wall of rubble, the far side of the tiny cave.

Geoff straightened up, coming away, shaking.

'She's—'

'No! We'll get her—she's not touched, only her legs.'

'Suffocated.'

'The air's getting in now. I'll get in and try and lift that timber, enough to get her legs out.'

Pat loosened out a hole big enough to climb through. Geoff flung the bricks and stones out to enlarge it, and willing hands scooped it away, the access getting rapidly larger. The fragile cave trembled, the dust spiralling up. Pat went in, delicate as a cat. Geoff saw the danger and signalled a 'hold it' message. He wriggled in over the wall, holding out his arms to get a grip under Marion's shoulders. He could only do it by feel, the light blotted by his own body, sensing Pat's groping beyond him, trying to find a hold under the timber. Pat was doubled up, his back hard against the angel. Geoff retreated, seeing the difficulty, and got the torch and brought it gingerly back in. He shone it for Pat, lighting up his searching hands, scraped and bleeding like his own, the gloves long since shredded and discarded. He remembered, in that stupid moment, America and Ruth and Ephraim—their momentous problems dwarfed to trivia—forgot instantly, searching with the torch to help Pat. They worked together without any need for words, desperate to free the trapped legs.

'Daddy,' Marion said.

'My little idiot.' He knew he was crying, but it didn't matter.

'I've got it,' Pat said. 'If you're—ready—'

Marion cried out once, and was silent. Geoff could hear Pat grunting and gasping, could virtually hear the timber moving by the noise of Pat's exertions. He got his hands under Marion's arms and pulled. She came some of the way screamed out again, and sobbed, 'Daddy, daddy!'

Geoff, heartened enormously, rested momentarily.

'Again,' Pat said.

'Try, Marion,' Geoff grunted. 'Your legs. Pull your legs—'

Pat made a noise like a discus thrower in the Olympics winning a gold medal, and Marion came to Geoff's embrace, landing a cloud of dusty hair in his face. The stones slithered and crunched underneath them, filling their nostrils with plaster dust. Geoff heaved again.

'Oh, daddy!' Marion got her skinny arms round Geoff's neck and he flung backwards, landing her like a fish over the top of the hole and on to the debris beyond. Eager hands reached for her, lifting her up.

Geoff groped up for the hole again, and found Pat on his way out, white and shaking.

'Christ, give me air!'

'Pat, she's O.K.! It's all right!'

They staggered out into the open, in a worse state than Marion. The crowd gathered round, beating them on the back in congratulation, everyone pushing and shouting, wanting to see where everything had been happening. The police pushed them back; the ambulance-men pounced to add Geoff and Pat to their collection.

'No! Damn it! What have you done with her? Where is she?'

Geoff pushed his way to the altar steps where Marion was lying on a stretcher wrapped in blankets. She was smiling happily.

'She's all right,' he said. 'You're not taking her away.'

'We're taking her to casualty.'

'What's wrong with her?'

'Shock, bruises.'

'She's coming home.'

'Yes,' said Marion. 'I want to go home.'

Alfred intervened, and the local doctor, and two police-men, and after a good deal of argument, the ambulance-men took their blankets and stretcher back and Marion got to her feet. Pat gathered her up in his arms. A newspaper-man took a photograph.

'We'll put her to bed,' Geoff said.

'I'll come and see she's all right,' the doctor agreed. 'To be on the safe side.'

'Yes, but she's not going away.'

Marion put her arms round Pat's neck and buried her face in his wet, gritty pullover.

'Pat.'

'What is it?'

'You're still here.'

The sun was shining and the marshes lay serene and steaming in the early autumn light. The wind was merely playful, the sky washed-out and cloudless, a perfect day for flying.

Geoff said, 'I'm afraid we've really messed things up for you this time.'

'No.'

They went into the house. Geoff, from habit, put the kettle on. Pat laid Marion on her bed and left her with the doctor and came down, sat in the armchair.

'I'm sorry,' Geoff said. 'Thank you, and all that. I can't say it exactly how I feel—too difficult. You know what I mean. Words aren't much good.'

'No. It's all right. I know—'

'Your hands—I'm sorry.'

Pat looked at them dispassionately. 'It's not everything, playing a piano.'

'Put it in writing.'

Pat grinned. 'It's too soon. I've never even said it before.'

'What are you going to do?'

'Go to sleep.'

'Have my bed. Go up now. I'll bring the tea up. I'll ring Ruth.'

By the time the tea was made, Pat was fast asleep. The doctor came down and Geoff gave him Pat's cup.

'She's quite all right. It's a miracle. I've given her a sedative. Her legs are bruised, nothing serious. If she just keeps quiet for twenty-four hours—well, I don't think there's anything to worry about. She was incredibly lucky.'

'Sugar?'

'No thank you. What was she doing there, in the middle of the night?'

'I don't know. I suppose the storm kept her awake. More than it did me.'

'Quite incredible, how that angel falling across the pew saved her.'

'She's done quite a lot for the angels in her time. Paying off a debt, you could call it.'

'It's a miracle.'

'Yes.'

'A tragedy for the church, but how much worse it could have been! You're a lucky man, Geoff.'

'Luckier this time than last.'

'Yes. You could put it like that. Liz didn't have luck on her side, I'm afraid.'

When the doctor had gone, Geoff poured another cup of tea and stood at the door, looking down the garden. His hands were shaking. Thinking of Liz, he was beyond tears, iced over. Even the tea would not warm him. And the doctor with his black bag of comforts was back in the village, sitting down to breakfast with his wife.

145

It was like watching a film, the effect of the sedative perhaps, not wanting to sleep, yet forced under, so that reality was blurred. With the doors left open, Marion from her bed could see across the landing to her father's bed, and Pat rolled up in the eiderdown fast asleep. A blackbird was singing on the roof and it was a lovely day. The sun fell in great slashes across Pat's form, turning all the grime on his face to gold-dust. He did not stir. Somebody came into the room very quietly. Marion recognized, even through the blur, a dark dress with red flowers on, dark hair, thin brown arms, reaching out. She lay down on the bed and took Pat in her arms, eiderdown and all, and laid her cheek over his, her hair falling over him. Marion saw Pat stir, unrolling from his cocoon, his arms reaching back. She saw his hands come slowly round Ruth's body, taking her, holding her, red and bloody, mixed up with the flowers. The blackbird was singing its head off.

Marion slept.

*   *   *

When she woke again the sun was much lower. It was very quiet. She lay still, remembering everything. She got out of bed and went to the window and saw the church with its lopped tower and the hole in the roof. Colin Pewsey was up there, covering it with tarpaulins, and quite a lot of people standing round watching. It was all very peaceful now, quiet and warm.

She crossed the landing and went to look out of the other window, remembering how it had looked in the storm. The tide was high again, but the serpentine loops of the river glittered idly, calmly, across the marshes and the reeds were flowering to the sunshine, standing up straight. The garden smelled of roses. Geoff and Ruth and Lud were sitting side by side on the deck of Geoff's boat, and Pat was in the river, naked, swimming all the dirt off him.

It was all over now, Marion could see. Her miracle had worked. She went back to her bed and sat with her knees pulled up, leaning against the pillows. She felt very hungry, and a bit shaky. She heard the others come up the garden and the sound of the kettle filling, voices talking quietly, laughing.

She called down. 'Pat!'

There was a silence below at the sound of her voice, then Geoff's voice, 'Do you want to come down? I'm making a cup of tea.'

'Yes, but I want to talk to Pat first.'

'All right.'

Pat came up.

'Privately,' she said.

'Of course.' He was dressed in the kitchen towel, still wet. He sat on the bed.

'You don't have to tell me,' he said quietly. 'You were praying for another miracle, and it happened.'

'Yes. How did you know?'

'The same as you knew we needed one.'

'Yes. It all happened at once. You were on the cliffs, weren't you, and the grave—the grave—'

'Went. I saw it.'

'I know.'

'How do you know?'

'I don't know that.'

'I don't think you should go in for miracles any more, Marion.'

'No. I shan't. We don't need them any more.'

'Well, not this moment.'

'I never shall again. They don't work how you expect.'

'You can say that again.'

They sat and stared out of the window at Colin Pewsey's

work party.

'We're going back to London,' Pat said.

'Not America?'

'Not this time, no. I feel differently about it—about quite a lot of things, actually. I'll tell Mick to go to hell and I'll have a quiet think. A long quiet think.'

'Yes. After all, you've got till you're about eighty, getting better all the time.'

'I suppose.'

He was silent for quite a long time, and Marion didn't say any more. She had never seen him look as he did now, completely at peace.

Ruth shouted up, 'I'm getting the tea. Are you hungry now, Marion?'

'Yes! I'll get up.'

'Ten minutes.'

'I'm coming.'

Pat got up, but stood hesitantly. 'There's something else,' he said.

'What?'

'Only for you, not to anybody else.'

'No.'

'When that grave went, I saw the bones. I got you one, for a keepsake.'

'Before they all went?'

'Yes. I nearly went too, you see. I was all mixed up with the cliff and the bones, scrabbling to stay on top. I just happened to grab one, and I held on.'

'Pure chance?'

'No. I wanted the lot, but I couldn't, could I? I shouldn't have been there at all. It was daft.'

'Where is it?'

'In the car.'

'I'll get dressed. I want to see it.'

'You remember what you said that time we walked there, that it might have been Swithin?'

'Yes.'

'Well, it's the tibia I've got. I asked the doctor, I showed it to him. He came back this afternoon to check on you, when you were asleep. And it's broken. Only half a tibia, snapped off in the middle.'

'A broken leg.'

'Yes.'

'And the church tower came down.'

'At the same time, yes. I saw it. I got back on firm ground, holding my half a bone, and the whole sky lit up and I saw the church tower fall.'

'That was me, praying.'

'You're some miracle-worker, I'll say that for you.'

'Yes.'

'It'll be safer in London. Don't do it any more, Marion.'

'No.'

It was a bit hard to take, thinking about it. Marion was still feeling fragile, and getting dressed was difficult, somehow. She decided to put the bone at the back of her mind for the time being. Pat got dressed too, in his filthy jersey and jeans, and they went down to tea.

It was scrambled eggs in the kitchen, with a cloth laid, and the evening sun streaming through from the open front door. It was very quiet and peaceful, nobody talking much. A great serenity pervaded the place, as if to compensate for the night before, the activity on the church roof finished, and nothing else yet started.

'I wonder what will happen to the church now?' Ruth said.

Curiously, Marion didn't feel she really cared. Perhaps it was the sedative. It didn't look very much different, once the first shock was over; there was an awful lot of it still left.

Her angels could still fly, pinned back by Ephraim's appeal. There were centuries still to come, and go, and nothing was in her hands any more. She had done what she wanted.

After tea she went out with Geoff to see Pat and Ruth off. Pat took a parcel out of the glove locker, wrapped in the old vest he used for cleaning the windows, and gave it to Marion.

'Thank you,' she said.

'Thank *you*,' he replied. He bent down and kissed her. 'For everything.'

She decided that she did love him very much. Ruth kissed Geoff.

They drove away and Marion stood with her father until the car had disappeared round the curve in the lane. They seemed to stand for a long time. Marion could feel the sun beating on her back; their shadows crossed the lane and tipped the walls of their cottage.

She glanced at Geoff. There was nothing she could do at that moment, she knew, just as sometimes he knew when to leave her alone, when it worked best. She went back to the church and lifted the heavy door-latch, and went inside.

'Thank you,' she said.

Not for everything, but for most things. Thank you for being alive. Thank you, Herbert, for saving my life. She went through the rubble to where Herbert lay across the front pew, and stroked the dust off the great ropy tendrils of his hair. She could feel the marks of Swithin's chisel under her fingers. She unwrapped Pat's oily vest and lifted out the bone.

'Swithin,' she said.

But it was Pat's face she saw, thinking of Swithin. Pat making music, as Swithin had made angels, the affinity binding them in her mind. And Swithin, for all that his bones, except one, were under the sea, was still here in his angels, and Pat was still in her life, in friendship.

It was strange, but she felt very happy, very much at peace. Trying to think why, in the face of all that had happened, it seemed to her to stem from the moment in her semi-consciousness when she saw Ruth go into the room where Pat slept and they had put their arms round each other. It had cut a cord, releasing her not only from a great burden of guilt, but showing her that, faced with fact, she had no regrets. The dream of someone coming as a substitute mother had been with her since Liz died, had crystallized, fleetingly, into possibility with Ruth's presence, but now that Ruth had gone she saw quite plainly that she felt the need no longer. The realization filled her with confidence and a feeling of freedom.

She thought of the things she wanted to do that she had neglected: see Flint and try his skateboard first; see if she could sew like Ruth and make herself a skirt. Ruth had said it wasn't a bit difficult. There was going to be a trip to London from school and she must ask Karen Norris if she would sit next to her in the coach. Karen was nicer than any of the girls in the village; she lived in Oldbridge. She had asked Marion to go back to hers for tea. She could come to mine too, Marion thought. Geoff would drive her home afterwards.

Everything was different now, somehow. She felt very contented, tired, like a cat in the sunshine. She walked out of the church and shut the door behind her.

Geoff was sitting on the front doorstep in the last of the sun, but he didn't look like a cat. Marion went and sat down beside him and put her arms round him.

'It'll be all right,' she said.

'I daresay. You can't win them all.'

'I'll look after you.'

'God help me, I reckon you will.'

'Truly. I'm different now. It will be better.'

'If you say so.'

He gave her a tired smile, turning his head, and she kissed and hugged him. She felt very strong and confident. The sun was a glowing halo over the trees beyond the church, slipping away fast, but the shadows were full of the warmth of the day, kindly and familiar.

'You're tired. You must go to bed. And in the morning you'll feel better.'

He allowed himself to be pulled to his feet. They turned their backs on the shadows and the silhouette of the stunted tower, and went indoors.